MB

LONG RIDE TO VENGEANCE

Long before meeting Diana, Matt Sutton had gunned down a wealthy rancher's bullying son to defend a former love's honour. Matt now wanted to forget it, but Reese Cantrell and his five bounty hunters wouldn't let him. They were after the price on his head, but with Diana they had an unexpected bonus. Matt had to act quickly, or the bounty hunters would have fun with his woman — and he would end up on the wrong end of a hangman's knot.

*Books by James Gordon White
in the Linford Western Library:*

COMANCHE CAPTIVE
RHONE
A MAN PURSUED

JAMES GORDON WHITE

◆

LONG RIDE TO VENGEANCE

Complete and Unabridged

LINFORD
Leicester

First published in Great Britain in 1990 by
Robert Hale Limited
London

First Linford Edition
published 2000
by arrangement with
Robert Hale Limited
London

British Library CIP Data

White, James Gordon
  Long ride to vengeance.—Large print ed.—
Linford western library
  1. Western stories
  2. Large type books
  I. Title
  813.5'4 [F]

  ISBN 0–7089–5758–7

Published by
F. A. Thorpe (Publishing)
Anstey, Leicestershire

Set by Words & Graphics Ltd.
Anstey, Leicestershire
Printed and bound in Great Britain by
T. J. International Ltd., Padstow, Cornwall

This book is printed on acid-free paper

To
Marie, James Sr and Solveig

1

Reese Cantrell drove the six men hard. He'd done so all the way from Texas to Colorado. It had been a laborious process, but they'd finally picked up their quarry's trail. If their luck held, the two should be in their gun-sights within a few more hours. But the immediate problem was to get off this narrow, icy mountain trail before the fading winter sun had set.

Shoulders hunched against the screaming, battering wind, the seven riders grimly continued on. There was nothing else to do, for it was impossible to turn around on the treacherous stretch. Already, each man's horse had slipped and all but skidded into the yawning chasm below.

Then disaster finally overtook them. Without warning, the last rider's horse slipped on the icy rocks, floundered, then shoved its wildly flailing, snow-packed hoofs into those of the pack horse. For an instant there was a struggling tangle, then man and horse were gone. Their hideous screams hung, echoing in the thin air, for long, agonizing moments after the rocks far below had done their work.

Only one man bothered with remorse. Naturally, he was the youngest, a handsome, clean-cut, blond youth of twenty, and had seen less of sudden, violent death than the others, who rode on with scarcely a backward glance, each silently thankful that it had happened to somebody else.

Another half-hour of painful progress brought them a welcome sight. Below the now descending trail was a snow-clad valley, shimmering brightly in the last glow of sunlight. And in it stood a solitary cabin, a ribbon of grey smoke rising from its chimney.

The hunt was finally over. All those long, hard months were about to pay off — and quite handsomely.

As the sun disappeared over the western mountains and a deep purple shadow moved across the valley floor, Reese Cantrell cautiously led his weary men down the widening trail. It would take a while, but before this night was done their quarry would be safely in their hands.

* * *

There had still been plenty of daylight when they came upon the deserted cabin, but they'd decided not to travel on and spend the night in comfort.

And now Matt Sutton and Diana Logan were taking advantage of its main comfort — a bed. It was lumpy and barely wide enough for the two of them, but, to Diana, it was heaven. Her tall, slender body refused ever to get used to sleeping on the hard ground. The tiny back room was away from the fireplace and the rusty pot-bellied stove in the main room, but the heat was slowly drifting in through the open doorway. At the moment, Matt and Diana weren't the least concerned.

Long honey-gold hair falling about her exquisite face in sweeping piles, Diana lay smiling up sensuously at Matt as her slim fingers slowly began unbuttoning her night-shirt. It was an old one of his that she slept in on the rare occasions when they found themselves indoors during their long trek to California.

Abruptly they became aware of approaching horses. The snow outside was only a few inches deep and did little to muffle the hoofbeats.

The sultry smile instantly vanished from Diana's lovely face as she sat up on an elbow and looked questioningly at Matt, who was now hastily pulling on his clothes. 'Could it be the owner of this cabin?' she asked, and modestly began to re-button her shirt.

'Who knows?' Matt said with a shrug, not looking up from his dressing. 'Stay put and I'll go find out.' The snorting horses were almost outside the front door. Pulling on his shirt, Matt grabbed his gun-belt from a chair beside the bed and went out, closing the door behind him.

Matt was almost to the cabin door when a deep, pleasant voice called, 'Hello, the cabin.' Despite the friendly tone, Matt stepped out with his pistol cocked.

Moonlight and the luminous snow did a fair imitation of sunlight, and Matt could almost make out the faces of the six riders beneath their hats. But he saw quite clearly the guns they all had trained on him. Framed as he was in the lighted doorway he made a perfect target.

'I'd say you've got the wrong man,' he said easily, thought every muscle was a coiled spring. 'I'm just squatting here for the night.'

'We've got the right man, Sutton,' said the same friendly voice, belonging to a tall man in a sheepskin jacket at the head of the group, 'Throw down your gun and stand there peaceable, unless you wantta be so full of holes you won't float in brine.'

Matt debated his chances, decided he didn't have any at the moment, then wisely uncocked his pistol and dropped it into the snow. He stood motionless, watching the men dismount a few at a time, their weapons never straying from him.

'That's showing good horse-sense,' the apparent leader of the group said amiably as the men advanced. 'Now let's all go in and stand by the fire for a spell.'

His mind on Diana, Matt reluctantly backed into the cabin ahead of the men. 'I'm not aware that I'm wanted for anything,' he said, subtly raising his voice to be heard in the back room. 'So why don't you put away those guns?'

'You got a short memory, Sutton,' the leader said, moving in ahead of the others, his pistol on Matt's belly. 'You killed a man four years ago in Uvalde, Texas.' His weathered, deep-lined face

6

broke into a sardonic half-smile. 'Guess you've killed so many you just plain disremembered him.'

Matt tensed, his jaw clenched. It was true, he'd almost forgotten the grim incident. As the men stomped inside he continued easing back, angling toward the fireplace and away from the back-room door. 'That was a fair fight,' he said evenly, drawing the men's eyes to him. 'Nobody said different.'

'Just the grieving father,' the leader said dryly.

Before Matt could reply, the back-room door opened silently behind the group and Diana, in her night-shirt, crept out on bare feet, pistol in hand. 'You men drop your guns and raise your hands!' she ordered sharply.

'Well now, I was wondering where you were, little lady,' the leader said, unperturbed, shifting his body slightly and craning his neck toward her. A wide grin creased his face at the sight of her.

Long, perfect legs braced apart,

Diana stared back determinedly at him through a tangle of golden hair fallen over her smooth forehead. The white, light cotton shirt, sleeves rolled up above her elbows, came to the middle of her straight, ivory thighs; the shirt-tails' inverted V-cut on the sides revealed her silky narrow hips. Her round, uplifted breasts rose and fell with her tense breathing, but the six-gun in her hand was unwavering. 'I meant what I said,' Diana reminded, her throaty velvet voice husky with emotion.

'I don't doubt your sincerity, ma'am,' the tall man said with an impressed nod, his eyes following the long line of her legs to her slim, precise ankles, then moving back up to her exquisite face, large blue eyes cold as a norther above her high, proud cheekbones.

Matt's stomach knotted as he abruptly noticed there were only five men inside the cabin. 'Diana — ' he began, only to be interrupted by the sharp sound of breaking glass as a rifle barrel thrust through a pane of the side window and covered Diana, who flinched, startled.

'Now I'd advise you to lower that gun and don't make a fuss,' the tall man said quietly. Diana hesitated, her eyes darting to Matt, then back to him. His long face open and sincere, the tall man completely turned to her and resumed, 'It's like this, ma'am . . . you'll get one, maybe even two of us . . . ' He nodded toward the rifle in the window. 'But Wiley there will shoot you dead, and the rest of us will be doing the same to Sutton. Then those of us left standing will take his body back to Texas and collect the reward.' He grinned and shrugged at the thought. 'In a way you'd be doing us a favour. The fewer of us, the bigger the shares.' His face became solemn, his voice utterly cold. 'Now I'm coming over and taking your gun. You just do whatever you have a mind to.' He started toward her with slow, easy strides.

Diana's determination faltered. She

looked past him to Matt imploringly. 'Let him have the gun, Diana,' he said, resigned.

'Best listen to him, ma'am,' the tall man said pleasantly, holstering his own gun and extending an open palm. Diana held her ground as he walked up and, meeting her eyes evenly, slowly reached out for her pistol. His long, bony fingers closed over the barrel and she reluctantly relinquished her grip. 'That's better,' he said with a relaxed grin. Diana lowered her eyes in bitter defeat. He stuck the six-gun into his gun-belt and, still smiling, made to turn away.

Suddenly he wheeled, lashing out viciously with the back of his hand, and swiped Diana across the face. The harsh blow resounded like a pistol shot inside the still cabin. Its force snapped Diana's head to one side and half spun her into the wall, hard. With a sharp, pained cry she weakly slid, sideways, down to the floor on rubbery legs.

'Damn you,' Matt yelled, his face

contorted in rage, and took a step forward. Instantly the four men barred his way, pistols cocked and ready. He froze, fuming in helpless frustration, fists clenched.

But the tall man's attention was on Diana, slumped against the wall. 'Don't you *ever* point a gun at me again, young lady,' he warned, his voice low and deadly.

Diana weakly raised her head and stared up at him with dazed eyes through a maze of long, dishevelled hair. A thin red trickle wormed from a corner of her mouth, but the hatred on her face made it clear that she was far from cowed by the brutal blow.

The tall man turned toward Matt and said, matter-of-factly, 'I don't believe in meanness for no reason. What I just did was a warning to both of you. She don't like being hit, and you don't like seeing it done. Now keep that in mind on the ride back. 'Cause every time you get outta line, she gets hit.' He shrugged. 'That goes for her, too.'

'Diana has nothing to do with what happened back there,' Matt said firmly.

'That don't make no nevermind. Old Man Goodsall's personal reward is five thousand dead, ten thousand alive — so he can have the pleasure of hanging you himself. Naturally, we got a strong interest in you staying healthy.'

'I might spite you and make you kill me.'

The tall man stared at him incredulously and motioned down at Diana. 'You'd leave this beautiful, helpless young thing all alone with this hateful bunch?' He shook his head and sighed in mock disgust.

Matt stared at the four hardcases in front of him, even the young, clean-cut one looked untrustworthy. 'What'll happen to her if I go peaceful?' he asked, resigned.

'Once we reach Old Man Goodsall's spread she's free to go, or stay and bring a box lunch to the hanging.'

'Don't listen to him, Matt,' Diana said defiantly.

'You have my word,' the tall man said gravely.

'And just who might you be?' Matt asked sarcastically.

'Reese Cantrell. Maybe you heard of me?'

Matt was damned impressed, but didn't give Cantrell the satisfaction of letting on. He nodded and remarked, 'Lawman turned bounty hunter.'

'Then you know I always get my man.'

'Not many of them ever lived to tell about it.'

'A few smart ones did.' Cantrell's smile was almost friendly. 'You and your girl have been smart up till now, just stay that way.' Matt stared back at him and said nothing. Though his smile remained, Cantrell's dark eyes were cold and threatening.

Then the tension was broken as the front door banged open and the man called Wiley tramped in. He was big, grizzled and mean-looking. Two bed-rolls were tucked under his arms, and two saddle-bags hung across his broad shoulders. He set his Winchester against the wall and kicked the door shut with a boot heel as he announced, 'The horses are in a lean-to out back. Everybody can go fetch his own belongings.' He turned to Cantrell. ''Cept you, Reese. I brung yours with me.'

'I surely appreciate that, Wiley,' Cantrell said politely.

Wiley began setting down his burden. 'Now that we got them two, when we gonna eat?'

'Soon as they're all tied up.'

'Then let's git at it.'

'I'll do the girl!' said one of the four men with Matt. He was a gaunt, wild-eyed man in his mid twenties, whose clothes hung on him like a scarecrow.

'All right, Ferret,' Cantrell agreed, 'but keep your hands to yourself.' He looked to Matt. 'We don't want to do nothing to rile Sutton — as long as he

14

behaves himself.'

His face a stoic mask, Matt stood passively as he was stripped of his gun-belt and his arms were jerked roughly behind his back. The clean-cut youth and a short, grubby, sullen man in his mid-years both kept their cocked six-guns on him while a huge, ugly, bearded brute in his forties tightly lashed his wrists together. Wincing inwardly, Matt turned his cold grey eyes to Diana and the one known as Ferret. It was small comfort, but he noticed that Cantrell was also watching them.

Rope in hand, Ferret anxiously waited while Diana eased herself up the wall to her unsteady feet. His wild, yellow cat's eyes followed her up, taking in every line of her willowy, statuesque figure. Then he stepped to her, his lowered eyes straining to see down the front of her shirt, its top two buttons undone, revealing more than a hint of her swelling bosom.

Aware of his eyes, Diana restrained

an impulse to clutch her shirt front and aloofly turned her back to him. She shuddered at the touch of his clammy hands as he began wrapping the long rope around and in and out between her slim wrists, imprisoning them snugly. Then she sharply tensed as his hands 'accidentally' brushed her firm, shapely buttocks. Ferret quickly looped the rest of the rope up her arms and tied it above her elbows. Diana grimaced and bit her lower lip as the rope was knotted so tightly her elbows touched.

Finished, Ferret turned Diana to face him and grinned, dropping his eyes to her breasts. She followed his gaze and her exquisite face darkened in anger. Her tautly bound arms forced her sculpted breasts to strain against her shirt. Then Cantrell's calm, stern voice claimed their attention.

'We'll put them in that back room for the night. But first take out their gear and check it for weapons.' Wiley headed for the room, but Ferret delayed, smirking at Diana. 'Ferret, give Wiley a hand,' Cantrell ordered pointedly. His tone sent Ferret reluctantly into the back room.

Diana looked to Matt, his face like stone. Although he was tied, the two men kept their cocked pistols trained on him. The bearded giant remained behind him, ready to grab him if he made a move. She flinched as Ferret whooped from the back room.

'Woo-ie! Y'all, lookie here what I done found!' He clomped out with Diana's saddle-bags in one hand and her gambling costume and black fish-net tights in the other. Wiley followed with Matt's saddle-bags. Ferret dropped the saddle-bags by Diana's bare feet and held up the skimpy, black one-piece costume for all to see. 'How about she puts it on, huh, Reese?' Though she'd never been embarrassed by her costume before, Diana flushed and looked helplessly to Matt.

Cantrell grinned wickedly. 'What do

you say, Sutton? Want her to parade around and amuse the boys?'

Rage, so intense that it brought bile to his throat, rose inside Matt. He was grimly aware of his impotency. All threats were useless. His hands knotted into tight fists, vainly exerting wrist pressure against his tight ropes. All he could do was hope that Cantrell wouldn't allow it to happen, for fear his bunch might become hard to control. Diana looked fetching in that shirt, but her gambling outfit was calculated to arouse men. And it sure wouldn't take much to set these hardcases off.

But Reese Cantrell seemed to be enjoying the thought of Diana in her scanty black outfit just as much as his men.

2

Reese Cantrell's long, bony face became sombre. 'We'll let it keep for now. Maybe she'll wear it to the hanging.'

'Aw, Reese . . .' Ferret groaned. Wiley gave a heavy sigh and disgustedly hurled Matt's saddle-bags to the floor.

'You heard me,' Cantrell said, an edge to his voice. He shifted his eyes back to Matt. 'I'm obliging you at the boys' expense — but you displeasure me, and she'll wear that thing all the way to Texas.' His eyes locked with Matt's, long and hard. Then he casually gestured toward the back room. 'All right, herd them in there and finish tying them for the night.'

The big, bearded man put a meaty hand on Matt's shoulder and shoved him forward. Diana shrank from

Ferret's grasping hand and shot him a withering stare.

'Wiley will take her, Ferret,' Cantrell said easily. 'You go find something to put over that busted window, before we all catch our deaths.'

'But Wiley done busted it!' Ferret objected, waggling an accusing finger.

'I told you to fix it,' Cantrell reminded him gently.

Ferret knew the danger behind Cantrell's soft tone and had the good sense not to argue. He dropped the stockings and costume on top of Diana's saddlebags, then, boot heels loudly scraping the floor, disappointedly moved away. Diana coolly turned and walked into the back room ahead of Wiley, who delayed to take several ropes from the big, bearded man as he and Matt came up. The three men trailed into the room and Cantrell ambled up and stood in the doorway.

Diana perched on the edge of the bunk, crossed her trim ankles and squeezed her thighs together, modestly trapping the front of her shirt-tail between them, as Wiley kneeled before her with the ropes.

'Put Sutton in that chair,' Cantrell ordered. 'We don't want the two of them getting too cosy.' He stood looking on while Mirabeau shoved Matt down in the chair beside the bed and deftly lashed him in place. He frowned as Wiley finished Diana's ankles and used the last rope to tie her legs, above the knees, taking the opportunity to inch his hands up her thighs. 'Wiley, if you're all done you can go settle in with the others,' he drawled softly.

Wiley's hands flew from Diana's thighs as though they'd been scorched, and he scrambled to his feet. Mirabeau fixed Matt's ankles to the chair's front rung and stood. Cantrell stepped into the room, clearing the doorway for the two men, then went to Matt and critically inspected his wrist bindings in the light of the low-burning lamp on a nearby stool. 'Be a waste of time fighting them knots,' he commented and moved to Diana. 'That goes for you, too, ma'am,' he said, after a moment's inspection. 'Now you just lay back and I'll tuck you in for the night.'

Diana's face made no secret of her suspicion as Cantrell gently turned her shoulders and lifted her legs up on to the bed. His hands were impersonal as he lowered her down on the bunk and arranged the small pillow beneath her head. Her distrust remained when he hesitated drawing the blanket over her and took a last admiring glance at her statuesque figure.

'You got nothing to fear from me,' Cantrell said and pulled the blanket up to her chin. 'I'll keep standing between you and my men,' he tucked the blanket around her, 'as long as you and Sutton don't act up.' He stepped back and directed his gaze at both prisoners. 'Most likely this'll be our only night indoors. Me and the boys are bone-tired, and are going to get a good sleep. I suggest you do the same.' He positioned the stool so that the lamp illuminated the two and then went out, leaving the door open.

For a long moment Matt and Diana remained motionless, listening to Cantrell's departing footsteps and waiting until his voice joined the incoherent droning in the front room, before pitting themselves against their tight ropes. It was a wasted effort that only brought self-inflicted pain. Diana was first to quit; Matt stubbornly persisted a few minutes longer.

As Diana lay letting the various hurts to her lithe body subside, she turned her head and looked up at Matt. 'Do you want to tell me about all this?' she asked quietly.

Matt's lean, ruggedly handsome face clouded thoughtfully. 'First off, Cantrell likes killing. He's said to have collected bounties on twenty-five men. Twenty of them were brought in slung across their saddles. He was a good lawman once, tamed a lotta tough towns, then something happened.' He shrugged. 'Anyhow, he's sure sunk low to be riding with this lot.'

It was uncomfortable lying on her snugly bound arms. Diana squirmed and, despite the hindering blanket, laboriously managed to twist on to her side. Breathing heavily from exertion, she said, 'I meant about what happened in Uvalde.'

'I killed that fella in self-defence.'

Diana waited, but Matt didn't continue. Sometimes his laconic trait made her want to scream. This was one of them. 'Surely there's more?' she prompted.

'It's a long story,' Matt replied evasively.

'You have all night,' Diana said lightly, 'and a captive audience.' She forced a smile and nodded down at the blanket covering her ropes, her attempted humour was wasted. Matt just sat there solemnly chewing things over.

At last Matt gave a prolonged sigh and relented. He knew only too well that once Diana's curiosity got aroused she wasn't about to let the matter drop till she was completely satisfied. 'Seeing as how you're in this, like it or not, I guess you got the right to know,' he allowed.

That's awfully big of you, Diana thought irritably. But, not wanting to sidetrack him, she only nodded and looked interested.

'Remember this happened before we ever met,' Matt said uncomfortably. Diana again nodded and held her silence. It wasn't easy to tell the woman he loved and wanted to spend the rest of his days with about another woman. But it had happened four years ago. His mind still recalled them though. He'd been twenty-four then and filled with the wildness of youth; otherwise, maybe he'd have thought twice about what he was stepping into.

★　★　★

He'd been warned that Ray Goodsall had laid claim to her, even though he was engaged to a wealthy cotton merchant's daughter down in Houston. Owen Goodsall was the biggest rancher in these parts, and nobody wanted to cross his only son. Ray got whatever he wanted when he wanted it. He was a dirtmean bully but no coward. He'd personally beaten hell out of two cowboys who'd flirted with Amy and crippled a third in a gunfight.

But none of that mattered in the least to Matt when he kept his afternoon meeting with Amy at the local hotel. They had been meeting on the sly for a couple of months, whenever he got a day off from the small spread he worked for. The rest of the time he found himself always thinking about the black haired and black eyed dance-hall beauty, and begrudging Ray Goodsall's hold on her. Once or twice, marriage even came to mind; but he wasn't ready to take on such a binding commitment. Amy was more like an obsession, and all their slipping around added extra spice to their lusty relationship.

It was late afternoon when Matt left the hotel with Amy, who was on her way to the saloon, and they ran smack-dab into Ray Goodsall. The inevitable had finally happened.

Goodsall was tall, a year or two older than Matt and a few pounds heavier. His tanned features had the cold, sculptured look of a statue. He was wearing a double-holstered rig, both guns tied down. His dark gimlet eyes were sizing up Matt as he addressed Amy. 'I thought I'd find you here with somebody.'

Amy went pale beneath her rouge and powder. 'Ray . . . ' she began.

'I'll deal with you later,' he snarled, his eyes not leaving Matt as they sought to intimidate him. He was disappointed to see that his hard stare had no effect. Matt stared back evenly, a hint of contempt playing across his lean face. 'Right now, I'm going to show this cowhand that he can't mess with my girl.'

Hoping to avoid a gunfight, Matt

took a step toward Goodsall who retreated a step, trying to keep the distance between them. Nobody wanted to shoot it out at close range. There was too much of a chance of the other man, no matter how bad a shot he was, putting a fatal bullet into you.

Apparently mistaking Goodsall's intent, Amy spoke up defiantly. 'We're through, Ray. There's no future with you getting married soon. From now on, I'm going to see anybody I want!'

'You heard the lady,' Matt said flatly, taking another step toward Goodsall.

'Shut the hell up, ranch-hand,' Goodsall snarled hotly. His eyes darted to Amy. 'We're not finished till I say so, you cheap tramp.'

A small crowd of passers-by began to gather off to either side in curious groups, but the woman and two men were oblivious. Amy gasped and bit her lower lip.

'You're gonna apologize for that, Goodsall,' Matt said, his voice soft but deadly.

'To a whore?' Goodsall said incredulously.

'Ray, please . . . ' Amy cried piteously, stung by his words.

'Then I'll make you,' Matt said, his hands curling into fists as he took another step forward.

Ray Goodsall's rage had already been primed and he was ready to make his play. He danced away, farther out into the street, and his hands hovered above his twin Colts. 'I'm gonna give it to you in the belly and watch you die!'

Matt hadn't wanted this; his intention had been to whale the tar outta Goodsall. But there was now no chance to get at him before he pulled those six-guns.

Simultaneously Goodsall's hands went to his gun-butts. That was his mistake. He was fast, but he slowed himself split seconds by going for both guns at once — something a real gunfighter would never do. A split second often decided who was left standing in a gunfight.

Reacting instantly, Matt's hand flashed to his holster. The big Colt filled his hand and swung up, training on Goodsall's chest a split second before his two guns cleared leather. There was no time for any fancy malarky such as shooting the gun out of Goodsall's hand or wounding him in the arm — not with two six-guns about to raise up and spit lead at him. Besides, Matt didn't trust his own skill that much, and the only woundings he'd ever witnessed in a gunfight had been purely accidental. He grimly squeezed the trigger.

The .44 bucked in Matt's hand as a blinding flame leaped from its muzzle. A round, blood-squirting hole appeared in the left side of Goodsall's chest, staining his white shirt, an instant before the loud pistol crack.

With a scream of pain Goodsall staggered back from the force of the bullet, then hunched forward, his tall frame swaying in a grotesque, loose-limbed dance of death. Both Colts discharged into the ground. One slug kicked up dirt and dust; the other slammed into a pile of fresh horse dung, which splattered him. The guns dropped from his hands. His mouth opened and closed, but blood instead of words poured out. Arms flung wide, he toppled backward and landed heavily, raising a cloud of dust.

As the dust settled over Ray Goodsall's corpse, Amy's soul-rending scream shattered the funereal silence. She raced forward, brushing past Matt, and went to her knees beside Goodsall. While Matt stared uncomprehendingly, she cradled Goodsall's head in her lap and sobbed wildly.

Holstering his smoking Colt, Matt ignored the murmuring crowd and walked to Amy's side. He stood for a moment confusedly watching her lovingly stroke Goodsall's dead face as she desperately repeated his name, as though willing him back to life. She was no faith healer. Then he leaned down and took her arm. 'Amy, it's over,' he said gently. 'You're free of him.'

'Let go of me you bastard,' she shrieked, savagely wrenching her arm from his hand.

'Amy . . . ' Matt began, but broke off as she raised her hate-filled face. Never before had such intense hatred been directed at him.

'Why wasn't it *you* instead!' she said, hissing the words. Slowly she turned back to Goodsall and tenderly brushed locks of black hair back from his glazed, unseeing eyes. 'He would have married me,' she said sadly. 'I *know* he would . . . and you killed him.' Eyes stabbing hatred, she again looked up at Matt. 'I hope they hang you!'

Her words snapped Matt from his stupor and brought crystal clarity. She had used him, been using him all along in hopes of making Ray Goodsall so jealous he'd marry her instead of that nice, rich, respectable girl in Houston. Because of her foolish scheme he'd killed a man for nothing. That could just as easily been him lying in the dirt, and it still would have been for nothing:

no way in hell would Ray Goodsall have ever married a saloon whore. Matt buried his hurt in rage. Rage so fierce it frightened him. He had to get away before he did something he'd regret the rest of his life. But first, he had to know the answer to one question.

He leaned down, grabbed her arm and viciously dragged her to her feet. She started to scream and struggle, then saw his deadly face and was suddenly afraid. 'How did Ray Goodsall know he'd find us together today!' he demanded. Amy gasped, shook her head and tried to recoil. Matt yanked her to him, his eyes boring harshly into hers. 'Tell me, dammit,' he shouted, fighting back the impulse to strike her.

Fresh tears forming in her eyes, Amy stammered, 'I . . . I sent word to him . . . '

Matt thrust her away in disgust. She tripped over Goodsall's outflung arm and fell beside him. Matt looked down at her and waved a hand to the corpse beside her. 'He was right,' he said, his voice cold and cutting, 'in everything he said about you.' She cringed as though he'd struck her and began sobbing. Matt felt no pity; he couldn't even stand to look at her. Feeling numb all over, he turned his back on her and walked toward his horse, tied to a hitch rail in front of the hotel. The silent crowd cleared a wide path for him.

Matt mounted and rode out of town with Amy's shrill curses following after him. No one made a move to stop him, not even the town sheriff. He rode straight to the Bar-D, drew his pay and then left Uvalde for good.

It was a long time before he could live with himself again.

3

For hours Matt Sutton drifted in and out of a fitful sleep, waking to gravely ponder his situation and set himself against his unyielding ropes. Toward dawn a plan came to him. He had to admit it was pretty frail, but it was worth the gamble. He turned it over in his mind for a while, to get things all straight. In order to build a convincing lie there must be an element of truth, and he certainly had that. Matt smiled in irony. Those two years he'd spent in Yuma Prison weren't entirely wasted after all.

When Matt was entirely satisfied with the plan, he decided to wake Diana. He hated to. She hadn't slept much more than him, and at the moment she was provided with a merciful escape from their dangerous situation. But it was important that she be able to back up his story if Cantrell questioned her. He looked across at her peaceful face, partly hidden by her long golden hair shimmering softly in the lamp's dim light. He called to her, his voice barely above a whisper. She woke instantly, her large eyes concerned and questioning.

Though there was a lot of snoring in the front room, Matt couldn't be sure all of the men were asleep. Not wanting to risk being overheard, he told Diana only the barest details. She could learn the rest when he spun the whole yarn.

'Do you think they'll believe it?' Diana whispered.

'When it comes to gold everybody wants to believe.' He grinned maliciously. 'There's nothing like the promise of it to set friend against friend.' Diana nodded, but didn't join him in a smile. 'Out on the trail anything can happen,' Matt said. 'We have to be ready to take advantage of the slightest mistake.'

'Reese Cantrell seems like a man who

doesn't make mistakes.'

'Maybe not, but sooner or later somebody will. Once we know each man's weakness, we can help them get careless.'

'Right now, I'm their weakness,' Diana said dryly.

'I don't want you to play on that unless there's no other way,' Matt said solemnly.

Arching her slim eyebrows, Diana looked up at the shadowy ceiling and then back to him. 'Matt, I've dealt cards in saloons for years. I certainly know how to handle men.'

'Just the same, you mind yourself around this bunch.' She nodded, but her lovely face had that familiar 'Miss Smarty-Pants' expression, which always reminded him of a teenage girl listening to her parents' unwanted advice. At twenty-six she didn't look much past her teens, while he looked every bit of his twenty-eight years and then some. He looked into her eyes and said softly, 'I don't want anything bad happening to you.'

Diana's expression softened, then became deadly serious. 'And I don't want you to hang.'

'I don't intend to,' Matt said, and forced a reassuring smile. Then they both stiffened as the men were heard reluctantly awakening.

After several minutes of groaning, snorting, coughing and throat clearing, several pairs of footsteps were heard approaching the back room. Matt nodded to Diana and they began the deception.

'I'm telling you we hafta do it, Diana,' Matt said, raising his voice to a normal tone.

'But are you sure you can trust them?' Diana said, playing her part. She managed to wriggle partly free from the blanket so that her willowy body would be the first sight that greeted their visitors.

Matt frowned disapprovingly. Damn it, he'd told her not to flaunt herself. Then he realized that she'd be seen soon enough when she was untied, and he continued the charade. 'You don't want me to be hanged, do you?' he said, his voice tinged with desperation.

'What's all this, a family spat?' Reese Cantrell drawled from the doorway. Mirabeau snickered behind him.

Feigning surprise, Matt and Diana looked to them. 'I got a proposition for you, Cantrell,' Matt said tonelessly.

'Matt . . . ' Diana began uneasily, shooting him a sharp glance.

'Be quiet, Diana,' Matt said sternly. 'I know what the hell I'm doing.' Diana meekly lowered her eyes and was silent. Now if he could only get her to behave like that when they weren't play-acting.

'I see you got her well trained, Sutton,' Cantrell said, with a hint of amusement. 'That's good.' He stepped inside the room. 'I truly admire an obedient woman.' Mirabeau lingered behind, his eyes ravishing Diana. 'Now what's this proposition of yours?'

Matt met his eyes and put just the right mix of sincerity and desperation into his voice. 'How'd you and your men like to be partners in a wagon-load of gold?'

'Gold?' Mirabeau exclaimed, instantly forgetting Diana's charms.

'Settle down, Mirabeau,' Cantrell said calmly, his eyes not leaving Matt's face. 'He'll say about anything to keep from hanging.'

'That's the only reason I'm willing to cut you in.'

'It don't hurt none to listen to him, Reese,' Mirabeau said eagerly. He elbowed Wiley away as the others, having heard the magic word, 'gold', began gathering around the door.

'I suppose not,' Cantrell agreed with a shrug. He went to the bed, excused himself to Diana, then moved her long legs aside and sat on the edge of the bed. 'All right, Sutton,' he said, again fixing him with sceptical eyes, 'fire away.' Mirabeau loudly shushed the murmuring group behind him.

'While I was serving time in Yuma Prison,' Matt said, carefully keeping his eyes on Cantrell's face, 'I got friendly with an old-timer named Pop McCarey. Seems during the war he and other Southern miners were sending gold from Colorado down to Texas for the Confederacy.' He paused, letting the fact sink in. Cantrell was looking for the lie, but this was the truth so Matt was on safe ground.

'I heard tell a lotta that went on,' Cantrell allowed.

'The Yanks got wise to them and were coming to close the mines and confiscate their latest shipment. Pop and the rest were warned in the nick of time. They sealed up the mines and cleared out with the shipment before the troops got there. It took some doing but they made it to Texas.'

'What's your point?' Cantrell asked impatiently.

Now came the lie. The truth had been established, and there was still more truth to come. 'There was one wagon that broke an axle and had to be left behind. It was sealed inside one of the mines.' Matt paused for effect, then said confidently, 'It's still there — and I know where to find it.'

'Let's go and git her,' shouted Wiley. The others set up an anxious clamour.

Cantrell turned his cold eyes on the group. 'Stop acting like a buncha Comanches. This discussion ain't over yet.' The men sheepishly fell silent, and he turned back to Matt. 'This old boy just up and told you, did he?'

'I saved him from another convict who had a knife. Not long after, he died of consumption. He knew I'd be getting out soon, and it was his way of paying me back.'

Cantrell mulled it over, then asked, 'How come nobody went back for that wagon after the war?'

'Pop was the only one in his bunch to survive the war. Afterwards, he got mixed up with rough company, and ended up serving a life sentence in Yuma.'

'What about the townsfolk? Could be somebody opened that mine and found the wagon.'

'That's not too likely. A short time after Pop and his men high-tailed it, the mines started playing out. The few that stayed behind were run off by Arapaho. With the war going on, the soldiers couldn't do much about it. But that was over ten years ago, and the cavalry's been strengthened.'

'That don't mean Indians ain't still about.'

'Indians or not, that's where we were heading.' Matt looked toward the group gathered at the doorway. 'Your men look like they can handle themselves. The more of us the better . . . just in case of trouble.'

'I ain't a-scared of no Injuns!' Wiley stated.

'Then you're dumber than you look,' Cantrell said, his eyes still on Matt. 'Mighty convincing story, Sutton. But I ain't known a convict yet who didn't learn to lie good in prison.'

'It's not a lie,' Matt said flatly.

'I say it is.'

43

'There's only one way to ever be sure.' Matt shrugged. 'Now if you'd rather throw away a wagon of gold for ten thousand dollars, go right ahead.' He met Cantrell's eyes evenly. 'But you'll wonder about it for the rest of your natural life.'

'He's right, Reese,' Mirabeau put in.

Cantrell considered, then a crafty smile came over his weathered face. 'We could make you tell, then take you back to Texas and come out here in the spring.'

'Only to find I'd lied to you.' Matt shook his head. 'I'm not doing any favours if I'm going to hang.'

Cantrell placed a hand on Diana's bare leg. 'Not even to stop us from turning your girl into something so ugly no man would look at her?' Diana tensed, her eyes wide.

Matt's guts twisted at the threat, but he kept a cool head. 'Like I said, you still couldn't be certain I wasn't lying. The area is honeycombed with mines. You could search till you're old and

44

grey and still not find the right one.'

Cantrell patted Diana's leg. 'Where is this town?'

'About a week's ride, depending on the weather.'

'Shucks, what's one more week, Reese?' Wiley said anxiously. The others chimed in, agreeing.

'If you're stringing us along, Sutton, the boys are gonna be mighty disappointed,' Cantrell said quietly. 'They don't take that too good . . . in fact, they get downright mean. So you'd best quit now, while there's no harm done . . . ' he squeezed Diana's calf painfully to emphasize his veiled threat. Matt met his eyes firmly and remained silent. 'All right,' Cantrell said with a weary sigh, 'here's how it's going to be. The two of you are still our prisoners till we find the gold. Then we'll divvy it up amongst us, and you can be on your way.'

'Your word on that?' Matt said, his eyes boring into Cantrell's.

'My word,' Cantrell said solemnly.

He smiled mirthlessly. 'Soon as I'm a rich man I sure as hell don't want the bother of nurse-maiding you all the way to Texas.'

'The split is fifty-fifty.'

Cantrell shook his head. 'Equal shares.'

'I'm the one who's cutting you in,' Matt protested, aware that he shouldn't give in too easily.

'I figure your life is worth giving up some of that gold for.' Matt opened his mouth to again protest, but Cantrell added pointedly, 'And having the privilege of being able to spend it.'

Matt scowled, pretending to mull it over, then nodded. 'All right, but Diana gets a share, too.'

'She's with you. She gets half of yours, or whatever you've a mind to give her.'

'That's not fair!' Diana flared, outraged.

'Maybe not,' Cantrell agreed with a shrug, 'but that's how it's to be.' He saw the two exchange frustrated glances.

'Now you two go getting greedy and the whole deal's off.' He eyed them hard. 'Ten thousand in hand buys ten million dollars' worth of talk.' He watched Matt and Diana's expressions slowly change to resignation. 'Now that we're all agreed,' he said in good humour, 'your girl can rustle us up some breakfast.'

'She ain't your servant.'

'It ain't going to hurt her none just this once,' Cantrell said, stroking Diana's long lovely leg. 'And it'll put everybody in a good mood to have some home cooking before we start this long ride to . . . what'd you say the name of this town was?'

'Vengeance,' Matt said quietly.

'Interesting name,' Cantrell commented with a nod. He stood and looked toward the men. 'Mirabeau, you and Virgil come untie them. The rest of you go on about your business.'

Mirabeau hurried ahead of Virgil and staked his claim on Diana, who turned on her stomach, denying him the chance to handle her body while getting at her bound arms. He leaned over her and went to work on her ropes. Scowling his disappointment, the short, grubby man unhappily went to Matt and began untying him. Cantrell stood back, hand resting cautiously on the butt of his Colt, and watched the four.

Matt sighed inwardly. Cantrell and his men had bought his story. Now he had more time and, with any luck, he might be able to stretch it out a few days more by not taking the shortest way to Vengeance. That seemed a good possibility, as none of the men had expressed any knowledge of the town. Every day out on the trail increased the chance of some mishap that might narrow the odds. The fewer to contend with when they reached Vengeance, the better his and Diana's chances were for coming out of this mess alive. He knew what was ahead when the men learned there was no gold.

4

Matt and Diana were the last to eat. Cantrell lingered over his coffee, his flinty eyes watching Matt's every move. Virgil and Ferret were also finishing up at the table. The other three men were packing their gear and none too subtly watching Diana as she returned to the table with a fresh pot of coffee. While she wasn't wearing her gambling outfit, what she had on still emphasized her tall, magnificent form. The shiny black leather pants fitted her like a glove and the matching knee-length, high-heeled boots were equally snug, as was the white flannel shirt, tightly belted to accentuate her narrow waist. A black scarf about her slender, ivory neck completed her outfit.

His mouth stuffed with food, Virgil grunted and shoved his cup forward as Diana came up. She obliged, moving between him and Ferret, and leaned over to fill his empty cup. Ferret couldn't resist the temptation to grab her taut buttocks. Diana reared with a startled gasp, spilling coffee on the table, then angrily whirled and poured a scalding stream down into his lap.

Ferret's giggles immediately became a series of pained screeches. Spewing partly chewed food from his bulging mouth, he released Diana and leaped up, brushing at his lap. 'Gawd damn you, bitch! You burned my — ' His words went unfinished as Matt leaned across the table and smashed him in the face. Ferret went down with a crash, tangled in his chair. Murder in his face. Matt charged around the table. Virgil calmly continued eating while the other three men started forward to stop Matt.

'Stay put,' Cantrell barked, smacking the table with an open palm. 'This here is a gentlemen's disagreeance.' The men halted in their tracks, bewildered. Cantrell pulled his Colt as Matt approached Ferret, who was struggling to untangle himself from his chair. His pistol had fallen from its holster and lay beside him. 'You want him, Sutton,' Cantrell said calmly, 'go ahead on. But you make a try for his pistol and I'll shoot you dead where you stand.'

Cantrell's words had little effect on Matt's rage. He was intent on hurting Ferret so bad that he or anyone else would think twice about touching Diana again. Ferret was pulling himself up with the support of the overturned chair when Matt reached him. He kicked the chair away and drove a fist down into Ferret's face, sending him sprawling flat on his back.

Scowling, Virgil turned indignantly to Cantrell. 'Reese, he ain't fightin' fair!'

'None of us do,' Cantrell said dryly, keeping his eyes on the one-sided contest.

Still clutching the coffee pot Diana shrank against the table, her wide eyes on the fight, as Matt ruthlessly battered Ferret every time he attempted to stand. The wild-eyed man certainly deserved it, as did all of the others. The whole pack was nothing but white trash as far as she was concerned, and, dead, the world would never miss them. She had seen Matt fight before and hated it. Not just out of fear for his safety, but because of what it did to him. He became a different person, a savage and frightening stranger.

Ferret dragged himself to the wall and, bracing himself against it, lifted his bloody face to Matt. 'Lemme up on my feet, dammit,' he hollered in frustration.

Matt stepped back and beckoned him up. 'Come ahead, boy,' he taunted. He let Ferret claw his way upright and then stepped forward and drove a fist deeply into his belly.

The air whooshed out of Ferret's lungs in a long sigh. Eyes bulging, he doubled over, clutching his belly and began puking his breakfast. Matt stepped to his side, seized him by the back of his collar and the seat of his pants and hurled him forward.

Diana and Virgil, taking his plate with

him, quickly retreated as Ferret, leaking a trail of vomit, came hurtling up and collided heavily with the table. He sprawled on top of it, head down, arms flung wide. Matt rushed up behind him and rammed a fist into his kidney. Ferret's head reared up with a sharp, gurgling scream. Matt grabbed a handful of his long, greasy hair and smashed his face down against the table. Ferret went limp, softly groaning and sobbing. Matt flipped him over on his back and began fumbling with the knotted rope holding up his baggy pants.

'You got such hot pants,' Matt said harshly, 'maybe you better take 'em down a spell and cool off.'

As the knot parted Ferret weakly tried to sit up, hands clawing at his pants. 'No!' he whined in panic. 'Leave 'em be!'

Matt brutally backhanded him across the face. Ferret's head slammed back down on the table and he lay stunned. Matt yanked the pants down to Ferret's boots, revealing his dirty long johns, and gave a strong tug. Ferret's body followed his pants and crashed heavily to the floor. Matt jerked the pants over Ferret's boots and left them inside out.

'That's what you were planning on doing to her,' he said, glaring down at Ferret. 'Now it ain't funny no more, huh, boy?'

Tears of humiliation running down his bloody cheeks, Ferret curled up, clutching at his pants. 'Damn you,' he sobbed. 'Damn you to fiery, almighty hell . . .'

There was a long uncomfortable moment as all eyes watched Ferret's pathetic figure, then Diana hurried to Matt. He put his arm around her shoulders and held her protectively as he glared at the other men.

Cantrell pushed his chair back with a loud scrape and stood. 'That was mighty entertaining,' he said, grinning. 'Sutton you're just as mean as they say.' He holstered his six-gun and ambled up to Matt and Diana. 'But don't go getting ideas that you can take on all of us.' He took Diana's arm and turned her toward the other men. 'Take a good look at her,' he began, only to break off as Ferret's sobs became louder. He shook his head in annoyance and kicked Ferret in the rump. 'Hush up, Ferret, I'm speaking.' Ferret quietened down and Cantrell resumed. 'Now, she's Sutton's woman and I want you to treat her right, here?' The men stared back at him stoically. 'I gave him my word nothing would happen to her if he co-operates and gets us to that gold. And, by damn, none of you are going to make a liar out of me.'

Knotting his belt, Ferret sat up and pointed at Matt. 'H-he shamed me!' he said between angry sobs. 'Shamed me in front of her and everybody!'

'He could have killed you, too,' Cantrell said softly.

Ferret sat trembling in rage, then saw his pistol and scooted to it. 'He ain't gittin' away with what he done!' His hand closed over the butt and started to raise the gun. Cantrell's boot stomped down hard on his hand. Ferret yelped and vainly tried to extract his hand.

Grinding his heel hard, Cantrell leaned over Ferret. 'You'd best start listening to me, son,' he said, his voice quiet and threatening, 'or else you won't live long enough to see the gold.'

'R-Reese . . . you're a-hurtin' . . . ' Ferret gasped, writhing and pounding the floor with his free hand.

Cantrell ignored him and, keeping his foot in place, pried the pistol from Ferret's hand. 'Now then, you apologize real nice to the lady, like a little gentleman.' Ferret defiantly shook his head, his wild, suffering eyes on Cantrell's boot. Cantrell applied more pressure.

'I . . . I'm sorry . . . ' Ferret muttered through clenched teeth.

'Louder,' Cantrell ordered, keeping up the pressure.

'I'm sorry to have bothered you, ma'am,' Ferret yelled.

Cantrell stepped back. 'Now that

didn't hurt, did it?'

Ferret sat up clutching his aching hand. 'Reese, you like to broke my hand,' he whined.

'Go saddle the horses,' Cantrell ordered sternly. He turned to the others. 'Virgil, Ennis, give him a hand.' The short, grubby man placed his empty plate on the table and headed for the door with the blond, cleancut youth. Cantrell watched Ferret, still holding his aching hand, start after them, then called his name. Ferret turned and he threw the pistol to him. 'Don't forget this.' Caught by surprise, Ferret grunted and doubled over as the heavy six-gun slammed into his stomach. 'You might want to shoot some varmint while you're out there.' Ferret turned and silently followed Virgil and Ennis outside. Cantrell turned to Matt and Diana. 'Don't take him lightly, Sutton. He aims to kill you.' He grinned sardonically. 'But I'll see that he doesn't try till after our business is done.'

'Mighty considerate of you,' Matt said dryly. He felt Diana's fingers grip his arm nervously. He wasn't afraid of Ferret, but this whole bunch put together did worry him some.

'Anything for a partner,' Cantrell said in mock good-humour. He turned, went back to his place at the table and picked up his cup. 'If there's any more coffee in that pot you're holding, ma'am, I'd sure be obliged.'

Diana glanced down dumbly at the coffee pot in her hand and was surprised that she was still holding it. She shook the pot, heard its contents slosh about near the bottom, then walked to Cantrell and silently refilled his cup.

★　★　★

Huge and golden, the early morning sun hung impaled on the towering, snow-clad eastern mountains like a bright star atop a Christmas tree. The thin carpet of snow in the quiet valley

58

shimmered in its unwarming light.

Wearing a heavy sheepskin-lined elk coat, Matt sat astride his horse while Wiley tied his gloved hands to the pommel of his saddle. 'Helluva way to treat a partner,' he remarked dryly.

Standing before the cabin door gripping Diana by one arm of her sheepskin-lined deer coat, Cantrell grinned broadly. 'We're not full partners till after I've seen that wagon of gold.'

'You'll see it, all right,' Matt said confidently.

'I'm counting on that,' his pleasant grin vanished, 'and so's your girl.'

Matt stared back at him without expression. Wiley shoved the reins into his bound hands and walked away. Matt's eyes remained on Cantrell.

Cantrell led Diana to her waiting buckskin and said, 'Give me your word that you won't try anything, and you won't be tied. Be a lot more comfortable riding.' Diana hesitated and looked to Matt, who stoically nodded. She nodded and started to mount. Cantrell caught her arm. 'I wantta hear you say it.'

Diana set her lovely lips in a tight, red line and regarded him scornfully. 'I give you my word,' she said coldly.

Cantrell nodded, pleased. 'And a lady never goes back on her word.' Undaunted by her withering stare, he started to help her mount. She aloofly shook off his hand and did so unaided. Cantrell walked to his bay and hoisted himself up into the saddle. 'Lead off, Sutton,' he called. 'But if you start feeling like doing something, just remember your girl is riding beside me.'

His face rock-hard, Matt turned his dun north and led the way across the small valley. The gelding pranced along, eager to be moving, but Matt held him to a fast trot. The silent group followed, also holding in their mounts, each of which seemed to want to take the lead. Matt turned in the saddle and looked back at the others. The two big men, Wiley and Mirabeau, rode behind and slightly to either side of him. Ferret, his yellow eyes blazing hatred from his battered, swollen face, tried to catch his eye. Matt disregarded him and directed his eyes farther back. Diana and Cantrell rode side by side. The tall bounty hunter was keeping his word and dividing his attention between Diana and Ferret. Matt was sure Cantrell would keep Ferret riding ahead of him for the whole journey. Virgil and Ennis were strung out in the rear. Matt turned back and continued across the valley.

Once more, Matt re-hashed his plan. It was a long, hard ride to Vengeance, even without the snow, and his plan called for taking trails that were even harder. He was endangering everyone, especially Diana, but there wasn't any other way. The longer they were out the better his chances of the odds narrowing. Greed had already been implanted in the men's minds and the supposed shares grew larger with the loss of each man. With any luck, they might start reducing the odds themselves. Right now he had the feeling that Ferret would be the first to make a dumb mistake. Hate usually caused a person to become careless. And Ferret had a good case of hate. He would subtly ride him and fan that hatred into a blood-mad rage.

They crossed the valley and started up a winding trail leading through snow-covered pines which had trapped and held the snow that had drifted under them. As they continued to climb, the steely-cold air knifed sharply into their lungs with every breath drawn. The sun gave off scant warmth and its reflecting rays threatened temporarily to blind all who looked at the snow for very long. Slowly they threaded their way through the shadowy pines and reached the top. Then they descended into a deep canyon between towering perpendicular walls. Matt gave the dun its head and let it make its own way. After a while the gorge bent and the walls flared out abruptly, allowing full sunlight to reach them again.

For hours they rode in near silence, speaking only when necessary, repeating the monotony of climbing one windswept ridge only to descend and then climb and descend another. Morning wore into day and still the sun's rays remained cool. During their rest breaks Matt was careful to remain docile. It was too early for the men to become careless, he needed first to lull them into a sense of security. He was now confident that none knew the way to Vengeance, as his meandering course had led them a good half-day's journey away from their goal and no one questioned his judgement. He'd continue on like this, then begin easing back in the right direction tomorrow.

It was nearing late afternoon when they rounded a bend and saw that the mountain trail narrowed precariously. Matt drew rein and sat studying the treacherous trail winding down to a forested valley.

'What are you stopping for?' Cantrell called.

'Come see for yourself,' Matt called back.

The others pushed their horses forward. Cantrell guided his horse past the others and halted beside Matt. He saw the stretch ahead and gave a low whistle. 'I've never been much for mountains,' he remarked dryly. 'Give me flat lands any time.'

Matt nodded down at his bound wrists. 'This is as far as I go like this.'

'If you're scared,' Cantrell said, his voice edged with sarcasm, 'one of the boys will lead your horse.'

'I'm not trusting my life to anybody,' Matt said flatly.

'Ain't you forgetting about her?' Cantrell asked, motioning back to Diana.

Matt swung his gaze to Diana, who sat her saddle wearily, then back to Cantrell. 'Something happens and I go over the side, you'll lose both the gold and the ten thousand.'

Cantrell eyed him narrowly and mused, 'Maybe we oughta just play it safe and take you back to Texas . . . '

Matt smiled thinly. 'And throw away a wagon full of gold?' He shook his head. 'You don't get rich by playing it safe.'

'I'm gambling on that wagon,' Cantrell said sternly. 'The ten thousand's a sure thing.'

Matt's voice came low and even. 'Cantrell, nothing is ever a sure thing.' They glowered at each other for a hard moment, then Cantrell relented.

'All right, Sutton, we'll do it your way.' His dark eyes gleamed shrewdly. 'But there'll be a gun at your girl's back the whole time.' He glanced over to Wiley. 'C'mon up here and ride point.'

'Why me?' Wiley asked disgruntled.

'Because I said so,' Cantrell said sharply. He looked to the blond youth. 'Ennis, cut him free.' He drew his gun and backed his bay away as Ennis prodded his horse to Matt's side and pulled a large bowie knife from under his coat. Cantrell cautiously kept his Colt on Matt while Ennis quickly sliced the ropes from Matt's wrists. Ennis backed off and Matt rubbed the blocked blood back into his half-numbed wrists. Cantrell motioned him ahead with the six-gun. 'Remember, gold or no gold, Ferret's just itching for a reason to do you. Try not to oblige him.'

Matt made no reply and nudged his horse after Wiley, who was timidly heading down the trail. The others fell in behind him and began the treacherous descent.

It was as Matt had predicted, thoroughly wretched. In silence, the group goaded their nervous horses down the twisting trail. Every so often a small avalanche of snow and stones cascaded onto the trail, spooking the horses and not doing the humans' wiretaut nerves much good either. An honest-to-God avalanche would sweep them off the trail in seconds and send them, screaming, to an unpleasant death on the snowy rocks far below.

About a hundred yards further on, Matt's horse stumbled. He desperately yanked back on the reins; the force brought the madly rearing dun away from the edge of the trail. The terrified horse reared again, lashing the air with its forelegs, and almost went over backwards. Matt quickly slid from the saddle, landed with shaky legs and clung to the reins till the frightened beast quietened down. He stared toward Cantrell and the others, who'd halted a safe distance uptrail from him, and saw Diana's horrified face. He managed a tight-lipped smile and called, 'It'd be best to walk the horses a spell.' He got no argument. The group gladly dismounted. Matt turned and, on still shaky legs, moved down the trail after Wiley, who'd also dismounted. The others followed at a respectable distance.

After about a quarter-mile, the trail became wider and easier. The group re-mounted and continued the downward journey with a greater sense of security. The sunlight was beginning to show signs of fading by the time they reached the bottom of the trail. Made careless by exhaustion and by relief at completing their harrowing ride, the men momentarily ignored Matt as they began dismounting and bunching up to talk. Matt took advantage of the moment of slackness and made his move.

Jamming his heels into the dun's flanks, he sent it lunging into the group. The horse's shoulder slammed into Mirabeau's back and knocked him forward into Virgil and Ennis. The three hit the snow in a confusion of arms and legs. Wiley lunged up at Matt and took a boot in the face for his trouble. The big man fell heavily against Cantrell, throwing him off balance and jolting the Colt from his hand. Matt leaned down, grabbed Diana's arm and swung her up behind him. He reared the dun at Ferret, who frantically backed away as its hoofs climbed the air, then whirled and galloped into the small valley.

Yellow eyes blazing in anger and excitement, Ferret ran to his horse, leaped into the saddle and, with a rebel yell, lit out after Matt. He was gonna take his pleasure now, and there was nothin' Reese Cantrell could do about it! Heedless of the confused shouts behind him, he yanked his Henry from its saddle holster and rode on.

Matt heard the waspish whine of a bullet passing above his head, closely followed by the crack of a rifle. Then there was a much louder crack from high above. Matt looked up at the towering mountain and saw the ice and snow near its summit begin to slip.

The shot had started an avalanche.

5

The sheet of white death began to move, thundering and rumbling down the mountainside. Matt heard Diana's terrified cry as she pressed the side of her face against his neck and tightened her arms around his waist.

Gaining, his face flush with wild excitement, Ferret snapped off another round. He cursed as it missed its mark and started to lever another shell into the chamber. Suddenly he became aware of the deafening sound above and looked up to see the sliding white mass cascading down the mountain. The sight of impending death shocked him out of his thirst for revenge. He saw Sutton cutting for an overhanging shelf at the foot of the mountain and, frantically sawing on his reins, headed after him.

The avalanche was gaining momentum at a frightening speed as Matt urged the floundering horse through the deepening snow. Then the dun broke out of the deep snow and on to firmer ground. They reached the sheltering outcropping of rocks with only seconds to spare. Matt and Diana leaped down and hugged the rock wall. He clung to the reins, keeping the wildly struggling horse beneath the shelf as the first bits of snow and debris showered down. The air was filled with thunder and then a thick white curtain obscured all.

Ferret and his horse screamed in unison as an engulfing ocean of snow came down in a terrifying rush, crushing them beneath its frigid, massive weight, and swept out from the base of the mountain in wave after spreading wave.

From their place of safety on the far side of the mountain Cantrell and the others sombrely watched the sliding snow slowly lose its momentum. An eerie silence finally settled over the valley. The men remained rooted in place, stunned by the awesome destruction they'd just witnessed, then Virgil broke the silence.

'That dumb Ferret brung half the mountain down on hisself and turned us into poor folks again!'

'I'd kill him fer that if'n he wasn't already dead,' Mirabeau said sourly.

'Let's go dig 'im up and make sure,' Wiley eagerly suggested.

'He's dead all right,' Ennis said. 'Ain't nobody coulda lived through that.'

'Sutton and the girl might have,' Cantrell said, hoisting himself up into the saddle. 'They reached that overhang before the avalanche hit.'

'You mean we's rich again?' Virgil asked hopefully.

Cantrell shrugged. 'Only one way to find out.' He started off while the others anxiously ran to their horses. Speculating amongst themselves, the men hastily mounted and headed after him.

The avalanche had changed the look of the mountainside, and Cantrell and the men forced their mounts through the deep snow toward where they remembered the rock shelf to be. The horses floundered, sinking chest-deep in places. Cantrell halted a short distance from the foot of the mountain and sat surveying the thick sheet of snow that seemed to stretch endlessly.

'How we ever gonna find 'em in that mess?' Wiley asked disgustedly.

As though in answer to his question the snow began to shift off to their left. Matt's horse crashed out into the open.

'Yahoo, we's gonna be rich yet,' hollered Wiley.

'Quit that ruckus,' Cantrell said sharply. 'You wantta start another snow slide?'

Wiley paled beneath his tan and sheepishly looked up at the mountain. The others warily followed his gaze. Cantrell prodded his horse toward the cave-like opening, but the men hesitated, uncertain. Then greed and curiosity won out over caution and they nudged their horses after Cantrell.

Matt emerged from beneath the rock shelf with Diana and his spirits sank at the sight of Cantrell and the men strung out behind him. Diana gasped and gripped his arm. He turned to her, his face a mask of dark gloom, and shook his head. There was no sense running, they'd only be ridden down. He saw the tears of despair welling in Diana's eyes and slipped his arm about her shoulders, holding her against him comfortingly. He noticed there were only five men now. Ferret was buried somewhere out there in the deep snow. The escape might have failed, but it had succeeded in removing the threat of that crazy permanently.

Cantrell reined in a few yards from the two and drew his Colt. 'That was a damn fool stunt,' he said tonelessly. 'You almost got yourselves killed, and for what? You're still stuck with us.'

'Maybe, but you're short one man.'

'I'd have had to kill Ferret one of these days. That avalanche just saved me the bother.' Cantrell met Matt's eyes coldly. 'I'm allowing you this one try. Now you should realize that you ain't getting away, no matter what you do. But if there's a next time, I'll have your girl staked out in the snow buck-naked. You got that?' Matt clenched his jaw so hard his teeth hurt. Cantrell motioned with his Colt. 'Start walking to your horses.'

Still holding Diana protectively, Matt began trudging through the knee-high snow.

★ ★ ★

Deep purple shadows were relentlessly smothering the last rays of sunset when the group camped in the protection of a stand of pines whose thick trunks and heavy boughs shut out the chill of the evening wind. A roaring fire was made and a meal prepared. Hands tied behind him, Matt sat alone on one side of the fire while Diana and the men ate. Afterwards, he was untied to eat and Virgil kept a cocked pistol on him. Diana tried to go and sit with him but Cantrell insisted they stay apart. She favoured him with a scathing glance and reluctantly plopped back down by the fire. Matt smiled across the fire. Diana forgot about Cantrell and returned his smile.

When Matt had finished eating, Virgil called Wiley over. The big man deposited Matt's saddle behind him, then tied him hand and foot. The group bedded down, each man taking a turn guarding him. Matt continually cat-napped, waking to struggle cautiously against his ropes under the cover of his blanket. He might as well have got a good night's sleep, for when dawn came he was still securely tied.

They broke camp and rode from the small valley. As they travelled through the monotonous white landscape, Matt subtly began working the group back on course. By noon they were headed in precisely the right direction. At least he'd managed to gain a day and a half by his unnoticed wandering, and had trimmed the odds. Now if only another catastrophe would strike and take out another man or two.

Unfortunately, it was an uneventful day. Matt was careful to remain docile, and his lack of sleep helped give the impression that he was a defeated man. Blinking and half-blinded by the brilliant sunlight and dazzling snow, they pushed on toward a new set of distant peaks.

It was late afternoon when they spotted smoke and crested a ridge to find themselves looking down on a trapper's cabin.

'What do you think, Reese?' Virgil asked, shivering in the wind that was kicking up with the approach of twilight. 'Sure be nice to sleep inside tonight.'

'That ain't going to happen,' Cantrell said, shaking his head. 'Now let's quit skylining this ridge and make for the thick timber over there.'

The disgruntled group obeyed, veering wide of the solitary cabin. Cantrell pushed them until the last ray of sunlight was disappearing over the mountain range. Then they made camp deep inside a pine forest several miles beyond the cabin. Playing it safe, Cantrell ordered the camp-fire to be small and low.

Again Matt and Diana ate last. Gun ready, Mirabeau impatiently stood guard over him. Matt still pushed it as far as he could in dawdling while he ate, allowing the blocked circulation to return to his half-numbed hands. He was going to need all the strength he could muster for an escape attempt tonight. There was no telling when such an opportunity would present itself again. If he and Diana could reach the cabin, it should be an easy matter to obtain a gun. Then he'd have a fighting chance and with luck —

'C'mon, Sutton,' Mirabeau grumbled, breaking into Matt's thoughts, 'don't be playin' with your food. It's already dead.'

Matt reluctantly finished the last few bites and held up the empty plate. 'Happy?' he asked dryly.

Mirabeau scowled and called, 'Hey, Wiley, come and do him up fer the night.'

★   ★   ★

The fire had died to glowing embers. Diana lay shivering as the cold seeped through her blanket. But it wasn't the cold that kept her awake; her mind was still on the trapper's cabin. She told herself that trying to reach it was as futile as trying to reach up and touch the seemingly near stars above her in the black sky. She turned on her side, drew the blanket tighter and irritably wondered why the guard didn't add more sticks to the fire. Then she saw that the blond youth had fallen asleep.

Excitement raced through her, jolting her to complete awakeness. Diana raised her head and looked toward Matt; he was staring back at her. They both knew this was their chance. Diana threw a cautious glance toward the men. They were all sleeping soundly. She edged from beneath her blanket, stood and, heart and lungs working like bellows, stole to Matt on soundless feet. She kneeled beside him, pulled off her gloves, and set herself to the arduous task of undoing the secure knot imprisoning his wrists.

Cold, haste and fear tried to thwart her. Diana almost jumped out of her skin when a dry twig suddenly popped in the fire. She and Matt froze like statues, their eyes going to the men. A couple stirred but remained asleep. Calming her frayed nerves, Diana forced her freezing fingers to continue picking and pulling at the hard knot. Then it broke apart.

Tossing off the rest of his blanket, Matt hurriedly sat up and rubbed his wrists. Diana flexed her bruised, half-numbed fingers and began on the knot holding his ankles. Her fingers weren't up to starting all over again, and Matt's hands needed time before they could function.

Time was something they didn't have.

Then a thought came to Diana. Quickly slipping on her gloves, she moved to the fire, picked up the end of a stick and held its small flame to the knot. In only seconds the smouldering rope parted. Matt grinned at her ingenuity and sat letting the circulation flood back into his legs. Diana helped him up and, moving as silently as possible, they slipped from camp.

When they were out of earshot of the camp, Matt and Diana broke into a run. They had to cover as much ground as they could before their escape was discovered. There was no sense trying to cover their tracks in the snow, the men knew exactly where they were heading. All they could do was hope they wouldn't be overtaken before they reached the cabin.

The faint yammering of excited voices reached them. The men were awake and would be on their trail in no time. Together, clinging to each other, they ploughed through the snow-covered boughs and ran on through the darkness. Matt kept their pace as fast as he thought Diana could sustain. Far behind the men's angry, searching shouts back and forth prodded them onward.

Soon Diana's long legs were becoming clumsy and weighted and her breath was laboured between her gritted teeth. Matt wasn't in much better shape. The hollering and crashing through bushes and branches continued behind them but didn't seem any nearer. A sudden missed step flung Diana face down in a drift. She lay there, arms outflung, breathing exhaustedly, making no attempt to stand. Matt dropped to a knee beside her and, taking her by an arm, said her name in concern as he hauled her up. She sagged, hung on him with her full weight for a moment, then regained her balance. The sounds drew closer; she pulled away with a nervous gasp, her large eyes searching the blackness behind them. Clutching her arm, Matt hurriedly led her away.

Trying to keep to a protective path of shadows, they plodded on. With each agonizing step of their shaky legs, their eyes seemed to blur with exhaustion that set their minds reeling, smothering all sense of direction. The unrelenting sounds continued behind them, but they were unable to judge if their pursuers were gaining.

Then the unexpected happened.

In mid-step, Matt's boot came down on something hard and unyielding and there was a sudden metallic snap. Agony shot through his leg, tearing a scream from his throat, and he sprawled headlong into the hard-packed snow. He lay still, aware only of the vice-like pain lacing his ankle. Diana's scream cut through his pain and forced his eyes open. An effort to sit up brought a sharper pain. He squeezed his eyes shut until it passed and his brain quit spinning. Matt felt Diana's tentative touch on his throbbing leg and again opened his eyes. His vision cleared some and he made out Diana bending over his leg. What he saw next brought a gut-wrenching panic.

A wolf trap clung to his booted ankle.

6

Teeth gritted against the agony, Matt weakly sat up and grasped the sides of the steel trap. The short chain connecting the trap to a heavy wooden stake rattled with his straining efforts. The sharp saw teeth remained sunk into his boot. They hadn't broken through the thick leather, but there was a good chance of that happening if he wrestled with it much more. Now he knew some of the sickening anguish and terror a trapped animal felt. He could well understand why many even gnawed off their own leg in their frenzy. He could still wriggle his toes inside his boot. That meant, despite the pain, his ankle wasn't shattered. Diana reached out to help, but he brushed her hand away.

'No,' Matt gasped, 'find something to use as a wedge.' Diana turned and frantically glanced about. Heavy footsteps crashing into the ice-crusted snow told that one of their pursuers was rapidly closing the separating distance. Diana leaped up and rushed to a small fallen branch. 'Forget that and get out of here,' Matt called urgently. She ignored him, picked up the branch and started back. Damn her stubborn ways!

There was a loud beating of branches and Wiley burst out into the faint moonlight. His gaze quickly took in the situation and a smirk came over his ugly face. 'Well now, what kinda varmint we done caught here?' He sidled forward, his eyes shifting to Diana, who stood rigid, clutching the branch. She immediately began warily edging toward Matt.

'Diana, run,' Matt shouted, looking helplessly from her to Wiley.

'Aw you don't wantta run from a big, handsome fella like me,' Wiley drawled, spreading empty hands for her to see.

'He's hurt, help him, can't you?' Diana pleaded.

'Sure enough,' Wiley agreed. 'You put down that stick and give me a hand.'

'Diana, don't,' Matt cautioned.

Wiley made a sudden rush for Diana. As he started past, Matt lunged, dragging his body as far as the short chain allowed, and caught Wiley's boot. The big man stumbled and smashed face-down in the snow. Diana stepped up and swung the branch down at him, swiping him across the shoulder as he rolled away from Matt's grasping fingers. She swung again, but Wiley, now on his knees, caught the branch and savagely jerked it from her hands. The force flung Diana to her knees. Wiley hurled the stick aside, scrambled to his feet and scowled down at Matt, stretched out before him, hands desperately straining to reach him. Laughing cruelly, he began kicking snow in Matt's face. Matt cursed, his hands going to his eyes.

'Stop it,' Diana screamed, angrily lunging up at Wiley. A strong shove of his huge hand set her back down hard on her buttocks.

Wiley moved around and booted Matt in the side. The brutal impact rolled Matt completely over in the snow, tightening the trap's sharp jaws around his ankle.

'How do you like them apples?' Wiley taunted. 'You ain't a-feelin' so mean now, are you?' Matt squinted up at him through pain-glazed eyes as Wiley drew back his foot to kick again.

'No,' Diana shrieked, flinging herself on Wiley and fighting like a wildcat.

Laughing in amusement, the big man easily warded off her mad blows and kicks, then twisted her arms behind her and pulled her to him. 'I favour a woman what fights,' he said. 'Makes a man know she's worth somethin'.' He lowered his head and planted a harsh, bruising kiss on her soft mouth. Diana uttered muted protests and shook her head, but he held the insistent kiss.

Diana sank her teeth into his lower lip. Wiley's head reared back with a strangled cry and his ironband grip on her wrists loosened. She stamped a boot heel down on his toes and ground, hard. Then she jerked a knee up between his legs. Wiley howled and staggered away, grabbing himself. Diana spat his blood from her mouth and started for Matt.

'Woman,' Wiley hissed between clenched teeth, 'I'm a-goin' to plant you like a tree!' Huge fist raised like a hammer, he shuffled toward Diana. She recoiled but wasn't fast enough to evade his other hand. Struggling, she raised an arm to ward off his blow.

'Wiley,' Cantrell's voice called, barking like a pistol shot. The big man froze, arm still raised. 'Let her go! Now!'

Wiley reluctantly released Diana and lowered his arm. She glared at him, then suddenly swung a roundhouse slap that jarred the big man right down to his boots. He bellowed and reached out for her.

'Leave it where it is!' Cantrell said sharply. He stalked forward, followed by the others.

'Please help Matt,' Diana said as Cantrell stopped before her.

'He brought it on himself,' Cantrell said, unconcerned. 'You two shoulda stayed in camp where you belonged.' He glanced at Wiley. 'You and Mirabeau see to him.' Wiley disgustedly trudged toward Matt with Mirabeau. Cantrell looked back to Diana. 'You disappointed me. A lady ain't supposed to break her word.'

'I'm sure you'll have other disappointments,' Diana said icily.

'From now on you'll be treated the same as Sutton.'

'I hadn't noticed any difference,' Diana said, meeting his eyes. Then she looked to Matt and the men.

Wiley and Mirabeau each grabbed an end of the trap and strained. Slowly the steel jaws parted and Matt scooted back, drawing his foot from the trap. The two men let go and the trap snapped shut with a chilling clang. Mirabeau moved to Matt and gingerly inspected his ankle.

'Don't feel like nothing's broke,' he announced.

Diana started toward Matt, but Cantrell caught her arm. 'I warned you about getting smart,' he said, his voice as chill as the mountain air. 'Now it's time for another lesson. Strip!' Diana stared at him with stunned eyes.

'Cantrell, if you — ' Matt began.

'Don't make any threats you can't keep!' Cantrell interrupted. He shoved Diana out so that all the men could see her. 'Start taking them clothes off, or I'll put a slug through Sutton's leg. Then there'll be no more worries about any escapes.' He drew his Colt and thumbed back the hammer.

At the sound of the ominous click, Diana hurriedly began unbuttoning her coat. She kept her eyes from Matt who lay stewing in impotent rage. Only Cantrell seemed to take no pleasure in watching; the others' eyes expectantly followed her fingers from button to button. She slipped off the heavy coat, dropped it to the snow, then, shivering at the frigid air, started to unbutton her shirt. Her gloves were a hindrance and she paused to remove them. She felt the men's impatience and had no desire to stretch this out. That would only make matters worse.

Murder and red rage boiled inside Matt, but he managed to hold it deep down in his guts. He hated the men and he hated himself as well. Diana was shaming herself for him, and he was helpless to stop it. His own foolishness over a woman four years ago was the cause of it all. How much more would he and Diana have to suffer before that memory was finally put to rest? He could see Amy's mocking face, hear her derisive laughter. Then a murmur from the men sent Amy back into the deep recesses of his mind, and he saw Diana drop her shirt on to her discarded coat.

Diana stood naked from the waist up before the men's admiring eyes and stared through them as if they didn't exist. Her trembling, near-frozen fingers clumsily tugged at her belt buckle.

She mentally cursed the delay. Then it was free, and she was working the snug, shiny black leather pants down over her slim hips, long legs, and halting at her boot tops. 'I'll need help with my boots,' she said tonelessly.

'That's far enough,' Cantrell said quietly, halting the men's rush to help her. 'Now just stand there.'

Shoulders straight, head held proudly, Diana tried to still her violent shivers as the icy wind caressed her goose-fleshed nakedness. She mentally damned Cantrell and his lot to the fieriest pit of hell. He had promised to stake her out in the snow if they escaped again. God, how would she ever survive it?

As if reading her thoughts Cantrell spoke up. His voice was casual, without malice. 'Seeing how we didn't bring any rope, we'll do things different this time.' He glanced about at the men. 'Each of you can step up and look at her good'n close — but that's all.' There were some disgruntled mutters but he silenced them sternly. 'I mean what I say. Now, Mirabeau, step on over there, and keep your hands to yourself.'

Matt glared up at Cantrell and choked back useless threats. Sure as night became day he was going to kill him and any of the rest left standing by the time they reached Vengeance. That wasn't a threat; it was a promise.

The stink of Mirabeau's buffalo coat made Diana more nauseous than the thought of the ordeal that lay ahead of her. She focused her eyes on the offensive coat and kept them there as he stopped before her and stood grinning like the town idiot. His hot, quickening breath was as foul as his coat and failed to warm her.

'All right, Mirabeau,' Cantrell said, after what seemed an eternity to Diana.

'Thank you, ma'am,' Mirabeau said politely; 'it truly was a pleasure.' Diana continued staring right through him, and also Virgil who anxiously took his place and looked her up and down like a kid at a candy counter. She was unable to halt the blush that started in the hollow of her throat and spread up into her cheeks and face, vividly contrasting her pale body. She was used to men's admiring eyes, but never while standing before them utterly naked. After a long, uncomfortable moment Cantrell ordered Virgil away.

Wiley walked up and slowly circled her, his hard, baleful eyes studying her from all angles. Fear knotted her stomach as he stopped in front of her and sneered cruelly. It look every ounce of will not to cringe away, covering herself, as he tauntingly brought his arms up, almost touching her, and crossed them over his chest. She tensed, clenching her hands at her sides into tight fists, and tried to keep her eyes off his smirking face while maintaining an impervious expression. Cantrell called Wiley away much quicker than the others, and he walked off chuckling to himself.

Ennis hung back, fidgeting and blushing selfconsciously, aware that all eyes were on him. Unlike the others, he showed no trace of lust and just stood there, twenty paces away, and stared at Diana sympathetically. The men hooted impatiently and he took a timid step forward. Again summoning her haughty expression, Diana tensely awaited his degrading presence. But the youth abruptly spun on his heel and quickly strode back toward camp. All but Cantrell laughed and jeered after him.

'Well, I guess the show's over,' Cantrell drawled. 'You can get dressed now.' While Diana hurriedly began dressing, Cantrell turned his attention to Matt. 'Your girl got off easy this time. But any more trouble and she *will* be staked out in the snow for an hour . . . and I'll really turn my men loose on her.' Matt stared up at him, granite-faced. He turned and beckoned to Wiley. 'You and Mirabeau help Sutton back to camp.'

'How come I'm always helpin' him?' Wiley grumbled. 'Don't even like him.'

Holstering his Colt, Cantrell walked

to Diana, picked up her coat and held it open for her to slip into. She angrily snatched the coat from him and stalked off, putting it on herself. He smiled after her then turned his attention to Wiley and Mirabeau as they began supporting Sutton between them back to the campsite.

7

On their return to camp Diana packed Matt's ankle with snow, to ease the swelling. As he was easing his foot back into his boot, Cantrell walked up with Ennis, who carried a handful of ropes.

'Yes sir, ain't nothing like a woman's touch to heal a man,' Cantrell said pleasantly. 'By morning you'll be good as new.'

'He can't walk on that leg,' Diana said, staring at the ropes in Ennis' hand.

'You'd be surprised what I've seen men do — men who were hurt a lot worse than him.' Cantrell motioned Ennis to Matt, who obediently put his hands behind him. 'This'll ensure that you get a good night's rest and don't go wandering off again.' Ennis finished with Matt's wrists and started to move to his legs, but Cantrell shook his head.

'You can leave his legs free tonight,' he pointed to Diana, 'but do her up real good.'

'There's no need, Cantrell,' Matt protested.

'She had her chance,' Cantrell said firmly.

'Since I'm to be treated the same as Matt,' Diana said coolly, 'do you mind if I sleep here?'

'Long as you're well tied, it won't do any harm.'

'Please, ma'am,' Ennis said awkwardly, as he kneeled behind Diana and touched her arm. Her icy eyes on Cantrell, Diana crossed her slim wrists behind her back and allowed him to bind them together.

'I'll send somebody over with your gear,' Cantrell said, and walked away.

'I'm awful sorry about this,' Ennis apologized, knotting the rope securely. He took another rope and moved around to Diana's ankles.

'He makes you do a lot of things you don't want to, doesn't he?' Diana asked, her voice hinting sympathy. Ennis gave an evasive shrug and kept his eyes on his work. Diana shot Matt a sideward glance; he already knew by the tone of her voice that she was up to something. Ennis tightly knotted the rows of rope and sat back. Diana tested her bonds and said, 'Cantrell will be very proud of you.'

Ennis dropped his eyes. 'Please don't mock me, ma'am.'

'I'm not mocking you, Ennis,' Diana said, taking the sting from her voice. 'I would never do that after what you did for me.' Ennis flushed and turned away. 'It took courage not to follow the others.'

Ennis turned back. 'You really think so, ma'am?'

'Yes,' Diana said earnestly. 'And my name is Diana.' She smiled sweetly, and Ennis looked uncertain. 'Matt and I want to be your friends,' Diana said, oozing warmth and sincerity. Ennis frowned, puzzled, and turned to Matt.

'That's right, Ennis,' Matt confirmed.

'Seeing as how we're going to be partners soon, we oughta be friends, too.'

'You mean you don't hold no hard feelin's toward me?'

'You're only doing what you're told,' Matt replied.

'Not for much longer,' Ennis said firmly. 'When we git that gold, I won't have to answer to nobody.'

'*If* Cantrell decides to give everybody a fair split,' Matt drawled. 'The sight of gold makes a man greedy.' Ennis's expression showed that he was chewing that over in his mind. He let things drop as he saw Virgil approaching.

'Ennis, what're you dawdlin' there for?' the short, grubby man asked irritably as he stomped up with Diana's saddle and blanket.

'I was only checking her ropes,' Ennis said defensively and made a pretence of further tightening the knot holding Diana's ankles.

'You tied 'em, didn't you?'

'Yeah, but — ' Ennis began.

'But nothin',' Virgil snapped. 'Git on back where you belong.' Ennis reluctantly stood. 'Go on, now!' Ennis took a lingering glance at Diana and moved off, his head and shoulders drooping slightly. Virgil dropped the saddle beside Matt's and began spreading the blanket. 'Don't be a-playin' up to that boy,' he grumbled.

'What?' Diana said, her big blue eyes wide and innocent.

'He ain't a-gonna help you none, so just stay clear of him.' Virgil picked up Diana, placed her on the blanket and folded one end over her. Then he moved to Matt and pulled his blanket around him. 'You see that she does, Sutton.'

'What do you care?' Matt asked.

'I don't like to see trouble when there's no sense in it,' Virgil said and stood. He glowered at Matt and Diana, then turned and stalked off, leaving them bewildered.

★ ★ ★

They were up at the first rosy light of dawn, and on the trail not long afterward. Morning hadn't changed Cantrell's mind and, like Matt, Diana rode with her wrists tied. Ennis was friendly and seized every opportunity to speak with Diana who was always careful to exude charm. Matt led the way and continued to turn their course slowly back toward Vengeance.

They travelled steadily for several hours, climbing farther into the mountain range. The trail curved upward through a belt of dwarf pine, then curved amongst slanting boulders, twisted back on itself, climbed again and entered a narrow gorge. They rode in single file, silent, wary eyes on the towering, snow-topped walls looming on either side. The memory of the avalanche that buried Ferret was still fresh in everyone's mind. An occasional rock or loose snow fell onto the trail, stretching taut nerves almost to breaking point. The impulse to make a mad dash was checked only by the certainty that the action would indeed bring down an avalanche. Nape tingling, Matt led the way and kept a tight rein on the dun; if the skittish gelding took it into his head to run the rest would follow. It was impossible to turn a horse around in the narrow corridor, so there was nothing to do but keep going.

For almost an hour they crept through the tortuous folds of the canyon. Then, very slowly, they made their way out of the cramped defile and out into the bright, cool sunlight. As soon as they cleared the canyon, Cantrell's bunch began talking like magpies, releasing their pent-up tension. Matt felt like whooping and hollering himself, but settled for a prolonged sigh. He turned in his saddle and looked back at Diana. Her face was wooden as she sat her horse between Cantrell and Ennis. She saw him and immediately brightened. They exchanged smiles, then Matt turned back and led the group on.

It was about noon when they came

across the recent tracks of an elk herd. Cantrell called a halt and addressed the group.

'This could be our only chance to lay in some fresh meat. Mirabeau, come with me. The rest of you wait here till we get back. Watch Sutton and the girl good. Keep them tied, and keep them apart from each other.' His dark eyes swept the group. 'They best be here when I get back.'

Virgil pointed up at several grey clouds tinged with black. 'Mountain weather usually don't hold fair too long. Maybe we oughta look fer shelter instead of settin' 'round in this open.'

Cantrell nodded and looked off toward a thick forest of pines on the far side of the small valley. 'Go squat over yonder.' He mused a moment, then added, 'What with these short days there probably won't be that much sunlight left by the time me and Mirabeau get back, so just go ahead and make camp.' He got no argument from the weary band. 'Let's go,' he said to Mirabeau, and they wheeled their horses.

'Wiley, you lead and Ennis and me'll watch Sutton and the girl,' Virgil said, watching Cantrell and Mirabeau ride off.

'Who done died and made you general?' Wiley asked, scowling.

'Sutton'll have a harder time gittin' past you than us,' Virgil answered tactfully.

'Guess he would at that,' Wiley agreed, pleased with his own importance. He took the lead; Matt followed and Virgil and Ennis rode on either side of Diana.

They made camp in a tiny clearing in the forest. Colt in hand, Virgil stood guard over Matt and Diana while Ennis and Wiley unsaddled the horses, leaving their blankets in place, so as not to chill the weary animals' steaming loins. After the horses were hobbled and fed, Wiley and Ennis began laying out the gear.

'You know, you ain't got a busted arm, Virgil,' Wiley said gruffly as he deposited Matt's gear beside him.

'Somebody's gotta watch them,' Virgil said defensively. 'Else Reese'll be hoppin' mad if'n they git away again.'

'Just tie 'em up good and we'll all keep an eye on 'em — and you'll be free to help with the chores.'

'Reese did say they was to be kept apart,' Ennis called, setting Diana's saddle on the other side of the clearing.

Seeing he was outnumbered, Virgil begrudgingly relented. Damn, he hated work. 'Awright, I'll go fetch some firewood. But anythin' happens with them, and I'm a-tellin' Reese it was your all's fault!' To his disappointment his warning fell on deaf ears.

'You stay and cover Sutton whilst I tie him,' Wiley said.

'I'll do Diana,' Ennis called, hurrying over to them.

'*Diana?*' Virgil exclaimed, eyeing the blond youth sternly.

Ennis nodded and said, unabashed, 'She's got a name, same as you and me.' He smiled and led Diana away.

Virgil stared after them in disapproval, then looked down at Matt. 'You just remember what I said last night.'

Matt sensed there was something more than envy behind Virgil's words. But what?

* * *

After the chores were out of the way, Ennis returned to Diana with a hot lunch and sat beside her while she ate. As they talked he learned how she'd left Texas right before the Reconstruction ended, with only a suitcase and a deck of cards to her name. She'd been dealing faro in a saloon when she and Matt first met. He'd fallen in with wrong company, robbed a stage and been caught. She'd waited a little over two years for his release, and now they were going to California to start a new life.

Diana wasn't like the other girls Ennis had known; she was so easy to talk to. He found himself telling how he'd run away from farm life and a stern, Bible-thumping father to become a cowboy and had fallen in with the famous Reese Cantrell. The more they talked, the deeper his feelings grew for her. He sensed she liked him an awful lot too. Maybe something good would come of all this. He determined that he was going to help her tonight when he was standing guard. It meant going against Reese, whom he truly hero-worshipped, but it wasn't every day that a man found someone like Diana.

8

Shivering under her blanket, Diana stirred in an uncomfortable sleep. A gloved hand suddenly closed over her mouth and brought instant awakeness. Her eyes flew open, wide and staring. A man's face leaned over from behind her and she felt his warm breath on her hair and cheek.

'Don't scream, Diana,' Ennis whispered, his lips brushing her hair, 'I want to help you.'

Diana nodded, recognizing the blond youth's voice, and forced some of the tension from her body. He removed his hand and motioned for her to be silent. She craned her neck and watched as he pulled off her blanket and withdrew the bowie knife from under his coat. While he deftly severed the ropes about her booted ankles, Diana's eyes nervously swept the sleeping men. Then she felt his hand on her arm, drawing her upright. To her surprise he neglected her bound wrists and helped her to her feet. 'What about Matt?' she whispered as he started to lead her away.

'I'll come back for him after you're safe,' Ennis said.

Diana shook her head and started to protest but abruptly tensed as one of the men groaned and stirred. She and Ennis stood rigid, staring toward Mirabeau as the big man shifted about, fighting his blanket. After a few heart-stopping seconds, he again lay still and resumed snoring. Ennis urgently tugged on her arm and Diana reluctantly accompanied him.

They quietly made their way out of camp and pushed through the snow-bowed bushes. Once they were out of sight of the camp Ennis, gripping her arm tightly, hurried their pace into the pines. As they continued, Diana became queasy with suspicion. Ennis stumbled on the uneven ground beneath the ankle-deep snow and released Diana's arm. She stopped, winded, and leaned against a tree.

'Surely we've gone far enough,' she gasped. 'Shouldn't you go back for Matt?'

Ennis turned to her and asked softly, 'Why would I want to do a thing like that?' His smile was truly frightening in the shadowy moonlight, as was the large knife in his hand.

★ ★ ★

Eyes heavy with sleep, Matt raised his head from his saddle and stared uncomprehendingly at Diana's empty bedroll. He drew a couple of deep breaths and cleared his sleep-fogged mind. His eyes darted about the camp. The kid was missing. Matt struggled up on to an elbow and looked around. The footprints of two people led away from camp.

Fear closed in around him as he remembered Virgil's warning against playing up to Ennis. At the time Matt had sensed Virgil knew more than he was telling, yet he'd allowed Diana to go ahead and be overly friendly to the youth. He pondered about waking Cantrell and the rest, then decided against it. This could be the mistake he'd been waiting for. No one was on guard now. If he could loose himself and find Diana and Ennis, he could overpower the youth and take his weapons. Then he and Diana would have a good chance against the others.

Bowing his back, Matt hastily began picking at the loose knot which imprisoned his ankles.

* * *

As Ennis approached, an insane gleam in his eyes, Diana gasped and pushed herself away from the tree. He lunged, caught her shoulder and shoved her back against the trunk, painfully mashing her arms and tied wrists between it and her body.

'Don't be scared of me, Diana,' Ennis

cooed, pressing his body against hers and gently tracing the outline of her cheek with the tip of his bowie knife. 'We're friends, remember ... good friends.'

'Y-yes, Ennis,' Diana agreed weakly, not daring to move a muscle, 'and you promised to help me ... '

'I surely intend to — soon as you tell me how much you love me.' He saw the fear and surprise in her large eyes and scowled. 'C'mon, tell me. Why else you been shining up to me?'

Somehow Diana found her voice. 'Ennis, we should go back now. Everyone will be wondering where we are ... '

'They're all sleepin',' Ennis giggled and lowered the knife. 'It's just you'n me ... all alone.' He replaced the knife in its scabbard. 'See — ain't no call to be afraid.'

'Ennis ... ' Diana began, only to have the rest of her words muffled as he pressed his mouth on hers in a hard, wet, demanding kiss. Though she didn't resist, Diana carefully kept her lips unresponsive.

Suddenly Ennis yanked Diana's coat open wide. She gasped, startled, and turned her head, breaking the kiss. He seized her shirt and also ripped it open, baring her naked breasts, then shoved both the coat and shirt back over her sharply drawn-back shoulders and down about her upper arms. The icy air on her bare flesh shocked Diana back to her senses. She started to scream, but Ennis' gloved hand clamped over her lips. His free hand dug a bandanna from his coat pocket. He quickly removed his hand and jammed the wadded cloth into her open mouth, muffling her scream.

'I didn't look at you good that time 'cause everybody was watching,' he said, pulling off his gloves. 'But now it's nice and private.'

While Ennis was momentarily distracted, Diana raised one knee and, shoving hard against the tree with her bound hands, drove straight for his groin. Eyes bulging, jaw slack, Ennis gave a high-pitched yelp and stumbled back. The sharp pain folded him in the middle and brought him to his knees. Diana left him there, clutching himself and whimpering while he slowly rocked back and forth, and ran for her life.

★　★　★

The knot unravelled and Matt's ankles were free. He threw a glance toward the sleeping men, then shoved himself to a sitting position and, raising his buttocks, painfully worked his bound wrists down behind him until he was able to step through them. Bringing his hands up in front of him, he stood and began silently following the two sets of footprints out of camp. He would worry about getting his wrists free later; now he must find Diana.

★　★　★

Fear numbed Diana's mind, blinding her sense of direction. The mouth-filling gag made breathing difficult and muted any cry for help. Running in ankle-deep snow with her hands tightly tied behind her was also a hindrance. But she knew she had to keep moving; Ennis wasn't going to stay down long. Shivering at the stinging, snowy touch of bushes and branches on her naked bosom and torso, she desperately pushed deeper into the forest.

Diana abruptly lost her footing in a deep drift around the base of a tree, but managed to fall to her knees and remain upright. She knelt there catching her breath for a long moment, then tensely glanced back over her shoulder, listening. Ennis wasn't heard or seen. The streaks of moonlight filtering through the shadowy branches plainly revealed her footprints in the snow. There was nothing she could do about that, but perhaps she could rid her mouth of the gag.

Opening her jaws wide, Diana pried

and prodded the saliva-soaked cloth with her tongue. The effort began to make her nauseous, but the cloth slowly spilled from between her lips. She lowered her head and spat out the rest of the bandanna. It plopped wetly on to her breasts, clung for an instant, then fell to the snow. She gulped a deep breath of icy air and quelled her nausea.

Suddenly someone was heard madly thrashing through the undergrowth. As the sounds grew, Diana staggered to her feet and ran. Her pounding heartbeat threatened to deafen her to the fast approaching danger behind her. Then she emerged from the dark shadows out into bright moonlight and found herself in a small clearing. She started across the luminous area, snagged a foot on a hidden fallen branch, and sprawled face down in the snow.

Slowly Diana raised her head and dazedly shook the snow from her face. The fall had almost knocked the breath from her and she felt too weak to rise.

She dimly became aware of her pursuer crashing through the pines and feebly rolled on to a shoulder in time to see Ennis enter the clearing.

Ennis halted and glared triumphantly at Diana's prone figure. Face distorted in maniacal fury, he stalked toward her. 'You shouldn't have fought me,' he hissed between clenched teeth. 'Now I'm gonna have to learn you good.'

Unable to stand, Diana, wide eyes glued on his menacing face, weakly shoved herself away, pushing with her legs and shoulder. There was no escape; he was almost to her. Diana gave in to her fear and emptied her lungs in a long, loud scream of terror.

★ ★ ★

As Diana's scream reached him, Matt halted, listening, the hackles rising on the back of his neck. He wheeled from the sets of footprints he'd been following and rushed in the direction of the fading scream. Behind him, he heard the distant sounds of the startled men waking in camp. Another scream pierced the still air. Matt ran on, urgently shoving through the snow-powdered bushes and branches. The deep snow and his bad leg tried to slow him, but he gamely staggered on, batting the various branches aside with his bound hands.

*　*　*

Hands about Diana's neck, Ennis straddled her narrow waist while she frantically writhed beneath him. 'I tried to be nice to you,' he said, his wild eyes staring down at her red, choking face. 'But, no, you had to go and be like all the others — a Babylon harlot, tempting men with your wicked smile and promises of sin. The prophets of old knew how to deal with your kind — and so do I!'

Flaring spots danced madly before Diana's eyes, blurring Ennis's hate-filled face and turning the full moon above his shoulder red. His raving voice seemed far away, almost obscured by her staggering heartbeat. She felt his fingers dig deeply into her soft throat, shutting off her air. The red spots merged, became a huge swirling mist.

She had to breathe soon or die.

Matt burst into the clearing, took in the scene in a single glance and charged forward without breaking his stride. Lost in rage, Ennis didn't hear him approach. Matt drew back a foot and booted him in the spine. Ennis screamed and reared, his hands leaving Diana's throat and grabbing at his back. Matt raised his cupped hands over his head and savagely smashed them down on Ennis' face, caving in his nose. Ennis sprawled on his back and lay dazed with agonizing pain. Matt kicked him in the ribs and sent him rolling away, staining the snow with his blood.

Coughing as she deeply gulped air into her bruised throat, Diana turned on to a shoulder and weakly struggled to sit up. Matt went to her, dropped to one knee and awkwardly helped her to push herself up on to an elbow. Coughs continued to rack her slender, half-naked body. Matt stared angrily at her open coat and shirt hanging loosely about her elbows and her ivory, goose-fleshed torso, shuddering uncontrollably from fear and cold.

'Diana . . . ' he began, then broke off and turned as Ennis's panicked cry interrupted him.

'My nose . . . ' Ennis sat up and gaped at his bloody hands which had been holding his shattered nose. 'You broke my face,' he whined, childlike. Then his body shook with intense rage. 'I'm gonna fix you for that!' He leaped up and yanked his knife.

Diana gasped and cringed. Matt desperately glanced about for some sort of weapon, as Ennis came toward him. Then there was a crashing of bushes and Virgil ran into the clearing. He stopped short, seeing the scene before him.

'Ennis, no!' he shouted and started forward.

Ennis continued advancing toward Matt. 'Virgil, keep out of this,' he called, sobbing in pain and rage. 'He busted me up, and I full intend to cut him good!'

Virgil turned, cupped his hands to his mouth and shouted, 'Reese! Come a-runnin'.'

As Ennis closed in, Matt scooped up a huge handful of snow and hurled it into his face. Ennis yelped and staggered back, momentarily blinded. Matt leaped up and began edging toward a partly covered branch on the fallen tree. Brushing the snow from his bloody face, Ennis charged, slashing wildly. Matt dove aside and Ennis rushed past, slashing only empty air. Matt rolled to his feet and ran toward the branch. Ennis spun and headed after him.

'Matt!' Diana screamed in warning, as Ennis bore down on him.

Waving his arms wildly, Virgil ran

between Ennis and Matt. 'Ennis, don't do — ' he broke off in a pained gasp as the knife slashed through his coat sleeve and bit into his forearm. He reeled away clutching his bleeding wound.

Virgil's distraction gave Matt time to reach the branch. He broke off a stout stick, whirled as Ennis closed on him, and brought it up just in time to catch the descending knife. Matt tried to twist the blade aside, but Ennis pulled it loose and rammed it toward his belly. Matt twisted away and the blade whisked past. Jabbing with the stick, Matt backed away from the savage blade.

'Ennis, you better quit it,' Virgil whined, cradling his injured arm. 'Reese ain't gonna like this one little bit.' He saw Ennis continue attacking Matt and threw an impatient look about the clearing for Cantrell and the others; he sure wasn't about to get in the middle of it again.

Chin down, gut sucked in, Matt dropped into a crouch and gave ground as Ennis pressed in. Glinting in the moonlight, the knife flicked forward like a snake's tongue, straight for his entrails. Matt leaped back and brought the stick down sharply on Ennis' shoulder; the impact almost drove the blond man to his knees.

'I'm gonna cut your guts out,' Ennis snarled in pain and frustration, stumbling about in the snow. The stick came at his head, but he ducked under it and bore in. The point of his blade ripped into Matt's coat, but failed to penetrate all the way through the heavy material. He heard the others coming and frantically pressed his attack, hoping to finish his opponent off before somebody could stop him.

The knife went for Matt's guts, but he blocked it with the stick. This time Ennis was ready. He caught the end with his free hand and tore the stick from Matt's grasp with the strength of a madman. Matt was jerked off balance, his full weight going on to his bad leg, which collapsed under him, and down he went on his back.

'Ain't nobody gonna save you now, Sutton,' Ennis hooted, his face alive with insane delight.

Matt lay helplessly staring up at death coming at him with a bowie knife. He heard Diana's scream and gravely realized it might be the last sound he ever heard.

9

As Ennis lunged down for the kill, Matt brought his leg up, caught him in the belly and sent him flying over his head. Ennis somersaulted awkwardly and came down hard, flat on his belly. For a long moment he lay still, then slowly raised his head, his eyes wild with pain and surprise, and yelled, 'Virgil! Virgil!'

Matt scrambled to his knees and turned toward Ennis. He was momentarily confused to see that the blond man had suddenly sprouted a humpback. Then Virgil knelt beside Ennis and gently raised him to a sitting position, revealing that the long bowie knife was buried to its hilt in his chest. The fall had driven the blade completely through Ennis's body, and its tip was the reason for the grotesque bulge at the back of his coat. Matt turned away, climbed to his feet and headed for Diana as Cantrell and the others entered the clearing. Before he could reach her, Cantrell grabbed his arm and yanked him around.

'You all right, Sutton?' he asked anxiously. Matt nodded. The tension left Cantrell's face. 'Damned if you don't take all.' He grinned broadly. 'Even with your hands tied, I should've known better than to worry about you.'

'Ennis could use some worrying.'

Cantrell shrugged, unconcerned. 'I didn't take him to raise.' Wordlessly Matt turned and walked to Diana. Cantrell stared after him, then walked to the group around Ennis.

As Matt sank down beside Diana, she gasped his name and awkwardly thrust her body against him. He draped his bound wrists over her neck and held her tightly. Though the chance for escape was lost, he had succeeded in narrowing the odds by one more man. He directed his attention to the group.

Wiley and Mirabeau stood looking on sheepishly while Virgil supported the dying Ennis in his arms. Cantrell came up and addressed the big men. 'You two get over there and keep an eye on Sutton and the girl.' The men hesitated, then Wiley gave a halfhearted wave.

'So long, Ennis.'

Mirabeau nodded and added, 'It's been a pleasure knowin' you.' Cantrell impatiently shoved him away and he and Wiley ambled off, tossing glances back over their shoulders.

Putting on his best grin, Cantrell hunkered down before Ennis. 'Well now, what happened here?' he asked lightly.

His pale face vividly contrasted by the dark, coagulating blood, Ennis sat clutching the knife hilt protruding from his chest with both hands. 'Hey, Reese, lookie,' he said, grinning wanly. 'I'm kilt.' He nodded toward Matt. 'That damn Sutton done me in . . . made me fall on my own knife.'

'Aw, Ennis, it was your own doin',' Virgil said. 'I told you to quit, but you just wouldn't pay me no mind.'

'He busted my face all up,' Ennis whined. 'Ain't no pretty girls gonna like me if'n I look like ol' Mirabeau.' He abruptly noticed the blood oozing from the torn sleeve of Virgil's coat. 'Hey, Virgil, you done cut yourself too?'

'You done it,' Virgil said simply.

'I'm awful sorry, Virgil,' he broke off in a violent cough, blood flowing from both corners of his mouth. 'Oh, God, I hurt . . . Reese, make it stop!'

'It will soon,' Cantrell said soothingly, 'don't fret.'

'I — I don't wantta die . . . I'm a-scared,' Ennis sobbed. 'I'm gonna die and burn in hell — just like my old man said.'

'Your old man's squirrelly,' Cantrell said in dismissal.

'N-no, Reese. He's a church deacon. He . . . he knows.'

'Whatever you say,' Cantrell said with a nod.

'That's right,' Ennis said, nodding back at him. A bewildered look crossed his face, then slowly became a grin.

'Hey, I don't hurt none. I can't feel nothing . . . nothing.'

'See,' Cantrell said pleasantly, 'what'd I tell you?'

'You're smart, Reese. I always said so, didn't I, Virgil?'

'You sure did,' Virgil agreed eagerly.

'Yes sir, Reese knows everything. He — ' A tremor suddenly ran the length of Ennis' body. He grabbed Cantrell by a wrist and pulled himself upright. Fear and disbelief on his twitching face, he stared pleadingly into Cantrell's face while his out-of-control mouth tried to form words. Then he abruptly went limp and fell back into Virgil's arms, the air escaping from his lungs in a long, eerie sigh.

Cantrell pried Ennis's fingers from his wrist and stood. 'I'm sorry, Virgil,' he said quietly.

Virgil gently lowered Ennis's body to the ground and looked up, tears forming in his eyes. 'I thought you didn't like him much?'

Cantrell shrugged. 'It don't hurt

none to be civil to a dying man.' He turned and walked toward Matt and the others, leaving Virgil alone in his grief. 'Awright,' he called, 'Ennis wants some burying.'

'Aw, Reese,' Mirabeau groaned, 'this ground's all froze up. 'Sides, we ain't got no shovels.'

'Yeah,' Wiley agreed, then pointed down at Matt. 'He done the deed. You oughta make him — '

'I ain't asking,' Cantrell interrupted sternly as he came up. 'I'm telling.' He eyed the two hard; they sheepishly dropped their eyes. 'If you can't dig a hole, pile some snow and things up over him. Now move!'

'Aw, you know how I hate to look at dead things,' Mirabeau muttered as he and Wiley disgustedly shambled away.

'And stay outta his pockets.'

They halted and turned back with innocent expressions. 'We wouldn't do a mean thing like that,' Wiley said indignantly.

'You heard me,' Cantrell said harshly.

The men turned and, grumbling to each other, shuffled toward Ennis and Virgil. Cantrell gave his attention to Matt and Diana. 'Now there's two less to split with,' he remarked casually.

Matt looked up, his arms still draped around Diana. 'The shares keep getting bigger all the time.'

Cantrell stared at Diana. 'As long as she's here, the odds are gonna stay in my favour . . . and don't you forget.'

Matt eyed Cantrell hard, then disengaged his arms from Diana and clumsily climbed to his feet. He started to reach down to help her, but Cantrell gently drew Diana up by her shoulders. He stared for an instant at her nakedness, then adjusted her shirt and coat about her while she watched him warily.

'You can fix it proper later,' he said impersonally.

Several wolves began howling back and forth. The mournful wails hung like a pall over the stark, moonlit area and set the group's nerves on edge. Virgil rushed up to Cantrell. 'Reese, you hear 'em?' he asked nervously, his head swinging back and forth across the clearing as one wolf answered another. 'They's a-talkin' about Ennis. They's comin' for him!' Cantrell only sighed disgustedly and stared at him as though he'd taken leave of his senses. Virgil grabbed the front of Matt's coat. 'Ain't that so, Sutton?'

Cantrell swatted Virgil's hand away. 'Better him than us.'

'But, Reese,' Virgil whined, 'they're gonna eat him!'

'Ennis don't give a damn no more, so why should you?'

'H-he was my friend.'

'Awright, soon as these two are bedded down for the night, you come on back here and keep Ennis company.'

'By my lonesome . . . ?'

Cantrell grinned nastily. 'What's the matter, Virgil? Ain't he your friend no more?' Shamed by his cowardice, Virgil lowered his eyes and fidgeted uneasily. Cantrell drew his revolver and took

Diana's arm. 'Start walking, Sutton, and don't even consider getting lost in the dark.'

Virgil stood staring after the three and wrestling with his emotions. The wolves sounded closer. That made up his mind, and he hurried after Cantrell and the prisoners.

★　★　★

It was a bleak morning, foggy and grey, with a threat of new snow before the day was done. Matt and Diana stood under Cantrell's six-gun while their horses were saddled.

'Where's Virgil?' Mirabeau complained, jerking the cinch tight on Diana's buckskin. 'He ain't never around when there's work to be done.'

'Reese!' Virgil's voice hollered through the fog.

'Yeah?' Cantrell shouted, not taking his eyes from Matt.

Pale and shaken, Virgil came stumbling through the wisps of fog. 'It was

135

awful . . . ' he gasped, breathing hard from running, and staggered to him. 'I went to pay my last respects to Ennis . . . ' He hunched over, head down, hands on his knees, gulping the thin air, ' . . . t-the wolves dug him up and chewed on him somethin' fierce. I like to throwed up all over at the sight . . . ' Cantrell edged away from him. Virgil slowly raised his head. 'He don't look like hisself . . . just a big mess of red, raw meat and bones.'

'Shut up, Virgil,' Mirabeau snapped, grimacing and rubbing his belly. 'You tryin' to make me lose breakfast?'

'We've heard enough,' Cantrell agreed. 'No sense talking on about something you can't do nothing about.'

'Wolves gotta eat, too,' Wiley chuckled.

'Damn you, Wiley, that ain't funny,' Virgil cried.

'I said this talk is over,' Cantrell said, a hard edge to his voice. He motioned to Matt and Diana. 'Now tie them on their horses and let's get moving.'

* ★ *

All morning they picked their way, single file, along the ragged mountainside, slowly moving above the forest and into the bald, craggy section between the timberline and the fog-shrouded high peaks. The higher they climbed, the colder it became; riding through wet, clinging fog didn't help any. Despite their heavy coats, all were shivering. Matt could even hear Virgil, riding behind him, as his teeth chattered incessantly. The morning dragged on, with no sign of the sun and its faint warmth.

Noon found them staring down into a mist-covered valley where a long procession of Indians was making their way across on foot and on horseback.

'Arapaho,' Matt commented. 'Looks like a whole tribe.'

'Smelly dog-eaters,' Wiley sneered.

'That don't hinder their fightin' none,' Mirabeau said.

'Appears they're moving down to a

warmer climate,' Cantrell drawled. 'That oughta leave this mountain to us.'

'Good,' Virgil said sourly. 'I hate Injuns.'

'They're likely to be the rest of the day crossing that valley,' Matt said, watching the distant forms constantly emerge and then vanish in the swirling mist. This was an unexpected stroke of luck: they had to go around the valley, adding almost another full day to their journey. He looked over at Cantrell. 'We'd better steer wide of them.'

'I reckon,' Cantrell agreed, and motioned him forward.

Matt turned his dun and led off; the others followed in single file. They cut back on the other side of the ridge and made their way along a narrow, snow-filled trail that skirted the valley and descended into the forest area. About an hour later they came to a gushing stream and halted to rest and let the horses drink.

Hands tied in front of them, Matt and Diana sat under a spruce and chewed strips of jerked venison. Lack of sleep and the hard ride had nearly exhausted Diana, and she ate listlessly. She leaned back against the trunk and closed her eyes, the unfinished strip of meat clutched in her black gloved hand.

'You should eat,' Matt gently prodded. 'You need all your strength.'

'I'm too tired to eat,' Diana said, wrinkling her nose, a cranky edge to her velvet voice. Matt wisely didn't push her. 'How much longer are we going to suffer through this hell?' she asked, not opening her eyes.

'A few more days, I suppose . . . ' Matt answered vaguely.

'White trash bastards,' Diana muttered irritably. 'I wish they'd all hurry and fall off the mountain.'

Diana rarely swore; Matt knew the constant hardships were taking a heavy toll on her. 'Yeah,' he agreed absently, hating himself for prolonging the arduous journey and the fact that his past folly was the cause of her suffering. Suddenly his thoughts were interrupted by Virgil's shout.

'You thievin' sumbitch. That belonged to Ennis.'

He looked toward the horses in time to see Virgil slam into Wiley. They fell in a tangle and rolled about in the snow. Matt glanced to Diana, who was watching the men. 'Things are starting to happen,' he whispered, 'just like I counted on.' She nodded, not taking her eyes from the men.

Virgil swung wildly, landing several blows. Wiley fended him off and bawled, 'Lookie, Virgil, you quit now, or I'm gonna have to hurt you!' Virgil kept right on swinging. His fist caught Wiley on the nose. The big man bellowed and hurled Virgil from him. 'That done it. I'm gonna give you what for!'

'Careful, Wiley,' Mirabeau laughed, 'he's a mean li'l cuss.'

Before Virgil could stand Wiley was on top of him. He flipped Virgil over and shoved his face deeply into the snow. Virgil thrashed madly, but Wiley held him down in the smothering snow and laughed at his urgent, futile struggles.

'That's all, Wiley,' Cantrell shouted, approaching, his face dark with anger.

'Reese, he made me good'n mad,' Wiley said, continuing to hold Virgil face-down. 'And I'm learnin' him better!'

Without another word, Cantrell walked up and kicked Wiley under the chin, sending him sprawling on to his back, stunned. Virgil raised his head and, spitting and gulping air, brushed the clinging snow from his face. Cantrell turned to Mirabeau. 'What's this about?' he demanded.

'Aw, he found somethin',' Mirabeau said, fidgeting uncomfortably, 'and was makin' out it belonged to Ennis.'

'It did!' Virgil said, crawling about on all fours, searching the snow.

Cantrell eyed Mirabeau hard. 'I told you two to leave Ennis's pockets be.'

Mirabeau lowered his eyes all sheepishly. 'We didn't — '

'Here it is,' Virgil yelled, and sat up

141

holding a plain gold cross and chain. Cantrell stepped to him and took the small cross. 'Ennis always wore that under his shirt,' Virgil insisted. Cantrell glowered at Mirabeau, who shrugged and looked away, scratching the back of his head. 'I was with Ennis when he took that off a Mes-can whore in Laredo,' Virgil declared, nodding firmly.

Cantrell's eyes swept the men contemptuously. 'I'm disgusted with the whole lot of you,' he said, and drew back to throw the necklace into the stream. His arm abruptly halted as something on the other side of the stream caught his eye.

It was a party of Arapahos.

10

There were ten of them, wearing heavy winter coats and robes of buffalo and beaver, approaching like dark spectres through the swirling mist. Their ponies' breaths rose like spouts of steam in the frosty air and added to the eerie illusion.

Cantrell slowly lowered his arm and stuffed the necklace into a coat pocket. 'Awright, everybody start laughing,' he said low, a wide grin fixed on his solemn face. 'Make like we've been funning.' He slapped Virgil on the back and laughed. Virgil forced a weak laugh. 'Go help Wiley up,' Cantrell ordered, low, still grinning.

'I don't like him no more,' Virgil protested.

'You like being dead?' Cantrell asked caustically. ''Cause that sure as hell is what's going to happen if they think we're divided and afraid of them.' Virgil quickly turned and started for Wiley, who was groaning and stirring. 'Take it slow'n easy, dammit,' Cantrell snapped. Virgil immediately slowed his pace. Keeping his eyes on the Indians, Cantrell said, 'Mirabeau, drift over to the horses and get your Winchester.'

'I ain't heard anythin' so funny in a coon's age,' Mirabeau chuckled, edging toward the horses.

'Sutton,' Cantrell called pleasantly, his eyes still on the nearing Arapahos, 'you and the girl stay put. And try not to let them see your tied hands.' Matt and Diana brought their knees up in front of them and pressed their hands into their laps.

Virgil grabbed Wiley's arm and helped him up. 'C'mon, Wiley,' he laughed, 'it's time to stand up and git kilt.' He pounded the big man on the back harder than necessary as they stood warily watching the horsemen.

'Least they ain't got no war-paint on,' Wiley said.

'That don't mean nothin',' Virgil said, and laughed and again swatted him on the back. Wiley scowled and sidled away.

An Arapaho halted on the opposite bank and watched the men stoically. Making a peace sign, Cantrell ambled up and stood across the stream from him. Their leader, a gaunt, hard-faced man in his thirties, returned the peace sign and began speaking in a guttural, thickly accented voice.

'We hungry. Much thirst, too. You got whiskey?'

'No,' Cantrell answered, his eyes hard. 'You got plenty of water in front of you if you want a drink.'

The Arapaho searched Cantrell's face and saw no hint of fear; he was one who would not be intimidated. His eyes swept the others. The men were all poised for trouble, hands within easy reach of their pistols. Then there was the moose of a man with the repeating rifle, which looked like a child's toy in his huge hands. This was not the time to fight. Still, he did not wish to leave without tribute of some sort, or he would look small in the eyes of his braves. 'Hunting bad,' he said. 'You have food for Injun?'

Cantrell considered a moment. The leader and two others had single-shot carbines, the rest bows and quivers filled with arrows. They were no match for six-guns and Winchesters but he'd just as soon avoid a fight if possible. Not taking his eyes from the leader, he called, 'Mirabeau, bring a sack of that jerky.'

'Reese, we ain't hardly got enough fer us'n,' the big man protested.

'Just do it,' Cantrell said, an edge underlining his cheerful voice. 'Virgil, bring Ennis's horse. We got no use for it.' While they waited, Cantrell noticed the Arapaho's eyes stray past him to where Matt and Diana sat. He tensed inwardly, knowing what was coming, and subtly let his hand inch closer to the butt of his Colt.

'White woman . . . hair like gold,' the

leader remarked thoughtfully.

Cantrell remained silent.

Mirabeau tromped up with the sack of jerky, followed by Virgil with Ennis's horse. 'Here, Reese,' he said and held out the sack.

'Tie it on Ennis's saddle and then send the horse across,' Cantrell said, watching the leader who was still studying Diana.

Mirabeau obeyed and Virgil swatted the horse's rump, sending it splashing through the icy stream to the opposite bank, where a brave immediately grabbed its bridle. Then the two lingered beside Cantrell.

The leader's eyes moved back to Cantrell. 'You want sell white woman?'

'No,' Cantrell said flatly.

'Injun give — '

'You give nothing,' Cantrell said stonily. 'But I give you something more — and then you *go*.' He dug the gold necklace from his coat pocket and held it up to catch the faint sunlight. Its reflection struck the Arapaho's face, momentarily blinding him. 'You like it?'

The leader turned his head aside. 'Like woman more.'

'It's this or nothing,' Cantrell said, his cold voice making clear there would be no more talk. He deliberately aimed the reflection into the Indian's eyes again. He calculated he could take him out fast, maybe get two more before the fighting started for real. Virgil, Mirabeau and Wiley would start shooting as soon as he got off his first round. They oughta bring the whole group down and maybe only lose one man. The leader held out his hand.

'Injun take,' he said sourly.

Cantrell grinned and tossed it to him. 'Wear it in good health,' he said dryly.

The leader caught the necklace, stared at it, then hesitated for another glance to Diana. His face showed his disappointment, but he wheeled his horse and led the group away.

Cantrell and the men remained ready, even after the Indians had disappeared into the mist. Cantrell released his tension in a long sigh and turned to the men. 'That's that.'

'Yeah, but let's git 'fore they change their minds and come back for another pretty,' Mirabeau said restlessly.

Cantrell nodded and called, 'Wiley, fetch Sutton and the girl.' Then he stood staring off into the fog, unable to shake the uneasy feeling that they hadn't seen the last of the Arapahos.

* * *

For what was left of the day, Cantrell rushed their pace, and Matt went along. He knew full well what was on Cantrell's mind. The same was on his. Now wasn't the time to delay, subtly to meander off onto winding trails that went nowhere. Not with the threat of Arapahos dogging their track. He sure hoped those braves hadn't gone back and gathered others.

They slowly climbed out of the timber and into the barren rock-strewn high ground, letting their mounts pick their own way over the deadly, ice-crusted snow. The cutting wind howled about them, making progress more hazardous. Despite their precautions, the snow still left signs of their passage. It was near dark when they finally rode into a small clearing hemmed in on three sides by jumbled rocks. The wind had died, but with night fast approaching there was frost in the air.

Cantrell stiffly dismounted, stretching and rubbing his lower back. His dark eyes swept the area thoughtfully. 'Virgil, Wiley, scout around for something to burn — and no more fussing between you.'

'Shouldn't we oughta camp cold tonight?' Mirabeau asked.

'No, I want a nice, big fire tonight.'

'Supposin' them Injuns see the smoke?' Wiley said.

'That's what I'm counting on,' Cantrell said quietly.

Matt eased his aching frame from the saddle then went to Diana and supported her down. She sagged heavily against him as her weary legs refused to hold her. Almost dragging Matt down with her, Diana sank to the ground and rested her arms and head on her drawn-knees.

'Sutton,' Cantrell called, 'you and your girl go set by them rocks over yonder, out of the way.' He pointed to a low tangle of rocks that climbed up into boulders.

Diana lifted her head, frowned irritably at the thought of moving an inch, but didn't resist as Matt gently helped her up. Together, they stumbled to the rocks and sat. She wearily leaned her head on his broad shoulder, sighed and closed her eyes. Matt sat watching the men move about the clearing as, like a general with his troops, Cantrell directed the placement of the camp-fire, horses and bedding.

As darkness began to close in about the clearing, Matt and Diana were summoned to the camp-fire, where they sat warming themselves while the men ate hurriedly. Then their wrists were freed and they were told to eat quickly.

'This might be the last supper for all of us,' Cantrell said, seeing Diana picking listlessly at her food. 'Dying is a little more bearable on a full stomach.'

'You really believe the Indians will attack tonight?' Diana asked; weariness made her voice seem indifferent.

'I truly hope I'm mistaken.'

'You considered giving us weapons?' Matt asked.

'I'm afraid you two might mistake me and the boys for Arapahos in the dark.'

'What happens to us if they get all of you?'

'You better hope they don't, because when I'm dead I won't have a care in this world.' Cantrell and Matt studied each other wordlessly. Then he said firmly, 'You have my word that if it gets right down to the end, one of us will see to it neither of you are taken alive.' He looked about at the rest. 'I expect you to honour that promise.' The men's eyes went from Cantrell to the prisoners and, one by one, they nodded. All knew the fate of an Arapaho captive; it was something no man would even wish on his worst enemy.

For a long moment a deathly pall hung over the clearing, and then it began to snow. The white flakes drifted down gently out of a grey and black sky. The fire hissed and sputtered, instantly dissolving the flakes that came near it.

'Tie them,' Cantrell ordered, 'then let's get up into the rocks.'

Matt hurriedly shovelled the last forkful of beans into his mouth; Diana left the remains on her plate untouched. Their hands were tied behind them and they were herded toward the rocks on the lee side of the clearing by Virgil and Wiley while Mirabeau and Cantrell delayed, feeding the fire and checking the hats and blankets, which were draped over saddlebags and mounds of snow, to give the illusion of sleeping bodies.

Once up into the rocks, Matt and Diana were seated a few yards apart, and their ankles tied. Then the men took up positions overlooking the clearing. His and Diana's lives were dependent on a swift, deadly ambush, and there was now nothing to do but wait and pray that Cantrell's plan worked.

★ ★ ★

The low-burning camp-fire was fighting a losing battle with the falling snow when the Arapahos finally came killing, and the small clearing resounded with their savage war-cries. Faces hideously painted, stripped of their heavy robes and coats for fast movement, the ten braves fired bullets and arrows into the sleeping forms and then descended on them with knives and tomahawks for the final butchery. On discovering the ruse the buckskin warriors' triumphant cries quickly became shrieks of rage and frustration.

Adding their rebel yells to the commotion, Cantrell and his men opened up on the group from the rocks with Colts and Winchesters. Caught in the open, the startled bucks went down like ripe wheat under a hail of hot lead, with scarcely a return shot fired. Their leader was hit in the face and chest and sprawled backward on to the camp-fire. He made no attempt to rise from the searing flames. Even after all of the Indians were on the ground, the withering gunfire continued.

Then an abrupt quiet settled over the clearing. Not a man stirred. All lay frozen in awkward postures of sudden, violent death. Very cautiously, Cantrell stood up and surveyed the dead.

'All right,' he said quietly, 'get down there and clean up the mess we made.' He pointed down at the camp-fire. 'Start with that roasting buck. There's nothing worse than the stink of human flesh.'

Mirabeau saw Virgil clambering down toward the clearing, then moved to Wiley, still crouched between two large rocks, and kicked him in the rump. 'C'mon, Wiley, you ain't no cripple.' He stared in bewilderment as Wiley toppled sideways and sprawled limply, his blood staining the snow. Mirabeau leaned over him and saw a bullet hole in the side of Wiley's head. 'Reese . . . ' he called weakly.

Cantrell walked up, and commented, 'Ricochet.'

'Them damn heathens,' Mirabeau roared.

'Cussing dead men won't help,' Cantrell said. 'That bullet had Wiley's name on it, and you can't change the fact.'

'Serves him right for robbin' the dead!' Virgil gloated from below.

'Shut your mouth, Virgil,' Mirabeau bellowed, 'or I'll bash you a good one.' He shook a meaty fist for emphasis.

Virgil levered a fresh round into his Winchester. 'You come try it, and I'll put a bullet through what you call a brain!

'I ain't a-scared of you, little man!'

'I ain't scared of you neither, you big

tub of buffalo chips.'

From his position behind Cantrell and Mirabeau, Matt tensed expectantly. Maybe Cantrell would abruptly find himself without any men. Then his hopes were shattered.

'Both of you shut the hell up,' Cantrell shouted, his voice filled with cold rage. 'We're too few to be arguing amongst ourselves. Now quit acting like a couple of kids in a schoolyard and get to work!'

This was the first time either man had heard Cantrell raise his voice in anger during the long months they'd spent together, and it had a very sobering effect on both of them. Virgil turned on his heel and strode toward the dead Indians, and Mirabeau took his rifle and began clambering down through the rocks. Cantrell watched them for a moment, then, confident peace had been restored, turned and walked to Matt.

'You look just a mite disappointed, Sutton,' he drawled.

Matt shrugged and squinted up through the falling snow. 'For a moment there, I thought it might get down to just us.'

Cantrell motioned to Diana, huddled watching them. 'And her,' he said pointedly. Jawline tight, Matt gazed up grimly. Cantrell shook his head, 'You don't want that to happen, because then I'd have to shoot her so I could give you my full attention.'

'Hey, Reese,' Virgil called, breaking the tension. 'This is the same bunch. The cooked Injun's got on Ennis's gold cross.'

'Best leave it on him,' Cantrell called lightly. 'It appears to be jinxed.' He turned back to Matt and mused quietly, 'Or is it this whole trek?'

11

The snow had stopped before the group rose at dawn, but the sky still looked threatening. They breakfasted in near silence and then broke camp. Matt led the way and continued to follow a straight route. There was no telling if any Arapahos would come looking for their dead tribesmen.

Soon icy winds kicked up, and the low-hanging grey clouds began changing to black. It was just a matter of time before the sky decided to cut loose with more snow. Matt kept his dun at as brisk a pace as the altitude and ice-crusted snow would allow. The others kept up the pace without complaint. Bringing up the rear, Mirabeau kept guardedly glancing back the way they'd come. No Arapahos made an appearance. The possible threat of snow and Indians wore on everyone's nerves as they climbed upward all morning.

By early afternoon they were working their way down through a tumble of snowy rocks toward a thick forest of fir and aspen when sleet began to fall, stinging their faces like a multitude of unseen needles. Riding behind Matt, Virgil hunched over in his saddle and futilely cussed the weather. Heads down to avoid its prickle, the five continued through the sheet of white. The strong wind became even fiercer, driving the sleet before it, floundering horses and doing its level best to blow the clinging humans right out of their saddles. At last they reached the forest, just as the sleet became snow flurries, whipped along by a hurricane-force wind. Cantrell pushed his bay forward and halted beside Matt.

'No sense going any farther today,' Cantrell yelled. Though they were only a few feet apart his voice was barely heard above the shrieking wind.

They camped under the thick

branches of snowflocked pines on the leeward side of a small clearing. The wind screamed through the trees and sought them out, hurling snow, snapping branches, and generally making things miserable. There was much to do, and few to do it. Still, Cantrell refused to take the chance of allowing the prisoners to help out.

'If this storm doesn't let up by morning we'll be stuck here,' Matt said desperately, as Mirabeau began lashing him upright against the trunk of a slender pine. 'That means we're gonna need all the firewood we can gather, to keep from freezing to death!'

'You leave that to me and the boys,' Cantrell said, covering Matt with his Colt while Mirabeau worked. Then he shouted so Virgil, who was tying Diana to another slender pine a few feet away, could also hear, 'Rub some snow on the knots holding their wrists.'

'It'll freeze the ropes,' Virgil shouted back, as he looped a taut rope down Diana's long, black leatherclad, legs and the trunk.

'That's the idea.' Then we don't have to concern ourselves watching them.'

'That's fer damned sure,' Virgil said, knotting the rope about Diana's booted ankles. He scooped up a handful of snow then moved behind the tree and rubbed it on the knots holding Diana's crossed, black gloved wrists together, while Mirabeau did the same with Matt.

Matt and Diana stood watching the men unsaddle, hobble, and feed the horses, then move around the clearing hacking off dead lower branches from the surrounding pines with hatchets taken from the massacred Arapahos. The men worked furiously, building up a sweat beneath their clothing, in spite of the freezing wind. The altitude and exertion soon sapped their strength, but Cantrell insisted they keep working. Leaving the captives untended, the three disappeared into the forest.

As the faint sounds of their hacking reached him, Matt pitted himself against the constricting ropes. The knots had indeed frozen, making any struggles useless, but his movement did stir his slow-flowing blood. He flexed his gloved fingers, wriggled his toes inside his boots, and kept shifting his weight from one foot to the other. He glanced over at Diana who stood motionless, her head drooped. She was exhausted from the long ride, but this wasn't the time to sleep. He shouted her name above the wind. She slowly raised her head and looked around. He told her to struggle, but she weakly shook her head.

'You've got to,' he shouted. 'And whatever you do, don't go to sleep — you might never wake up.'

Diana said something that was lost by the wind, then feebly stirred in her ropes. After a long, painful moment, she gave up and stood shivering as the wind whipped about the clearing, flinging snow on them. She spat out some flakes and said something that was again taken off with the wind, but judging by her dark expression Matt knew it was far from ladylike.

Cantrell and the men staggered back and forth from the forest with their loads. Though Matt didn't give a damn about them, he began to worry that the men might collapse from exhaustion and dehydration and never get up again, leaving their captives to slowly freeze to death. It wasn't a very comforting prospect. Already he was shaking like a leaf and his teeth were clattering like a telegraph key. He had to admit relief when he saw Cantrell lug a heavy dead branch into the clearing and abruptly fall on his face. The tall man wearily struggled up, stood breathing gusts of steam for a spell, then called it quits when Virgil and Mirabeau stumbled out of the woods on either end of a long, thick log.

A roaring fire was built and then Matt and Diana were freed from their trees, heated knives severing their frozen knots. Their wrists were re-tied in front of them and, barely able to move, they were half-dragged, half-carried to the fire. Seated across the blazing fire, its dancing flames casting weird yellow patterns on their strained faces, the three men and their two captives hugged the warmth.

Coffee, beans and salted beef were heated, along with the frozen water in their canteens. The group ate silently, without enthusiasm. Even after they'd finished, they remained at the fire's edge, almost scorching their clothing while relishing the unaccustomed warmth.

Bone-weary, they bedded down around the fire. Matt and Diana's hands were fastened behind them, then their ankles were secured and the ropes connected to their wrists, holding them in fairly taut hog-ties. Cantrell had added the extra precaution since Matt's display of dexterity the night when he'd almost freed himself and gone after Diana and Ennis. As Virgil and Mirabeau started to cover them with blankets, the nearby howling of a wolf was heard above the light wind.

'Why don't he hush up?' Virgil muttered, placing the blanket over Diana. Another wolf answered, also nearby.

'They's one of the loneliest sounds I ever heard,' said Mirabeau. He tossed the blanket over Matt.

'I keep seein' Ennis after what they done to him,' Virgil said, absently tucking the ends of the blanket around Diana. The howls continued. He suddenly leaped up and yelled, 'Shut up, damn you, shut up.'

'They ain't gonna listen to you, Virgil,' Cantrell said quietly, watching him from across the fire.

'Them things is gittin' on my nerves!' Virgil said, staring out into the darkness.

'They're on everybody's nerves,' Cantrell said, 'but hollering at them don't do no good.' Virgil gave a wave of disgust and walked away. 'Go check on the horses while you're headed that way,' Cantrell called after him.

'He's not gonna be much use if he keeps actin' that a-way,' Mirabeau said, standing and looking toward Cantrell.

'He's just brooding about Ennis,' Cantrell said in dismissal. He looked to Matt, who'd been listening with interest. 'Don't get to smirking, Sutton. The longer we're out here, the more danger it is to her.' He motioned to Diana and grinned harshly.

Suddenly the horses' frightened whinnies were heard, along with savage growls. Then came Virgil's nervous shout. 'Reese, come quick. Wolves is attacking the horses!'

Cantrell was up in an instant, his hand flashing to his Colt. 'Mirabeau, grab your rifle and come on!'

'What about them?' the big man asked.

'They're tied good, ain't they?'

The loud crack of Virgil's pistol sent Mirabeau running for his rifle without replying. Cantrell bolted toward the horses. Matt and Diana tensely stared after the two as the sounds of wolves, horses and wild gunfire became more urgent.

'Matt, what if the wolves attack us?' Diana asked fearfully, staring in the direction of the horrible sounds.

'They won't come near this fire,' Matt reassured her. He began to twist about, testing his ropes. 'Let's worry about getting loose while they're gone.'

It took no time for the two to discover that they were tied as securely as each previous time.

* * *

The pale moonlight filtering through the snowcovered branches gave an eerie, unearthly look to the horses' area. The confused scene was a primitive battleground of men and horses against a large, starving wolf-pack. Dark blood stained the stark whiteness. The air was filled with shots, curses, savage growls, dying yelps and whimpers, and shrill whinnies of fear and pain. Horses reared and stamped at their attackers' with hobbled forelegs, or kicked their hind legs like mules. Some kicks connected, crushing ribs and sending furry, yelping bodies flying. The three men banged away; Mirabeau with his rifle and Virgil and Cantrell with their six-guns. Gunsmoke and clouds of steam from the breaths of men and animals alike threatened to obscure the battle.

Virgil laughed in mad glee at every wolf he downed. 'Eat my friend will you, you furry bastards,' he hooted. His pistol clicked empty and he clawed more shells from his gun-belt, dropping several into the snow in his frenzied haste.

Boots, paws and hoofs kicked up more mist into the murky air. A horse sank its long sharp teeth into a leaping wolf's neck and shook it viciously, like a terrier with a rat. With a toss of its head, the horse sent the dying wolf sailing into the air. It hit the ground heavily and, too weak to move, lay spreading its lifeblood across the ground with every panting breath. Another horse's kick crushed a wolf's skull with a sickening crunch.

A wolf went for a horse's underbelly, intent on ripping it open. Mirabeau charged up and smashed his rifle butt down on its back. The wolf's spine broke in two with a sharp crack. The beast whimpered and tried to crawl away, dragging its back legs through the blood-stained snow. A pair of shod hoofs crashed its skull to a pulp and ended its suffering.

A huge, shaggy black wolf rushed Cantrell as his gun clicked empty. He whipped his forearm up to protect his exposed throat an instant before the beast leaped at him. Sharp fangs dug into his sheepskin coat, but before they could rip through to his flesh Cantrell bashed the wolf's skull open with his pistol butt.

The remaining wolves turned tail and retreated into the pines, leaving the snow littered with their dead and dying. 'Damn your eyes, come back and fight,'

Virgil screamed. Caught up in his blood-lust, he ran after them.

'Virgil, get back here,' Cantrell shouted. Virgil paid no heed and plunged into the dark forest. 'Ignorant fool,' Cantrell muttered, then went to inspect the horses. On the way he shot a wolf that was trying to bite its own tail in its mad pain. His act was in anger, not mercy. Other shots boomed from the pines as Virgil pursued the fleeing wolves.

Mirabeau shook his head and grinned. 'That Virgil is sure havin' hisself a time.' Cantrell muttered something unintelligible as he moved about calming and checking the horses. Mirabeau took a sweeping glance at the dead wolves. 'Hey, Reese, whatta you think these here pelts should bring?'

Cantrell shook his head in dismay. Here they were on their way to a wagon full of gold, and the big dumb galoot was fretting over some measly wolf pelts. 'Do what you want,' he drawled, 'but I can't see going through the mess and bother of skinning something I can't eat.'

Mirabeau screwed up his face in hard thought. But before he could reach a decision Virgil's distant voice screamed through the pines.

'Reese . . . Mirabeau, help! They's a mess of wolves all around me!'

'I knew it!' Cantrell said disgustedly, raising his eyes to the sky.

Then Virgil's agonized screams rang from the forest.

'Hang on, Virgil,' Mirabeau bellowed, 'I'm a-comin' fer you.' Clutching his Winchester, he went charging into the pines like a bull-moose. Cantrell remained behind with the horses. He didn't want to chance any wolves returning.

Following the screams and growls, Mirabeau threaded his way through the pines, batting branches aside and sending snow flying. He came on a small open space and saw Virgil rolling, kicking and screaming as six wolves darted back and forth, jaws snapping viciously. A seventh wolf had its teeth fastened in his crooked arm and was trying to get at his face. Roaring like a grizzly, Mirabeau rushed forward, Winchester blazing. Three wolves fell spurting blood, then the rifle was empty. Reversing it, Mirabeau gripped the smoking barrel in his gloved hands and charged to Virgil's side. The flailing rifle stock caved in ribs and skulls and knocked wolves flying.

A wolf jumped on Mirabeau's back, its teeth snapping at his collar. Mirabeau casually reached back over his shoulder, caught the beast by the scruff of its neck and flung it to the ground. Before the stunned wolf could rise, the big man leaped into the air and came down on top of it with both feet. Ribs cracked and splintered under the massive weight.

Mirabeau leaned over Virgil, who continued sobbing and screaming, weakly trying to defend himself even though the danger had passed. He rubbed snow on Virgil's bleeding face and the icy shock seemed to restore his senses. His screams became anguished moans and he trembled violently from head to foot.

'God . . . what they done to you?' Mirabeau said, sucking breath between his teeth and wincing at the bloody rips all over his body.

'M-Mirabeau . . . ' Virgil whispered, 'they h-hurt me bad . . . '

'You're gonna be real fine, Virgil,' Mirabeau said, working up a confident smile to hide his concern. Virgil moaned and whimpered as he raised him up. 'Don't you fret,' Mirabeau said, draping him over a brawny shoulder. Then he picked up his rifle and started back to camp.

He surely hoped Virgil wouldn't die on the way. The thought of toting a dead man all that distance was plumb upsetting.

12

Matt had wriggled free of his blanket and was painfully hitching himself toward the camp-fire when Diana nervously gasped his name. He craned his neck and saw Cantrell, Colt in hand, striding forward ahead of Mirabeau who was carrying Virgil slung over one shoulder. Matt's heart sank; the chance of escape was gone.

'You had to go getting smart, didn't you?' Cantrell said, his voice low and angry as he stalked up to Matt.

'Want me to kick 'im fer you, Reese?' Mirabeau asked, coming up behind Cantrell, and glowering down at Matt.

'Ain't you forgetting that any of his smartness is supposed to be taken out on his girl?' Cantrell said with a tight smile. Mirabeau fidgeted sheepishly, reluctance plain on his face.

Matt shoved himself up on to an

elbow. 'Touch her and — '

'Don't go getting on your high horse, Sutton,' Cantrell interrupted. 'I'm letting the matter drop, 'cause I was begging you to try something by leaving you alone. But this is the last time.' He eyed Matt narrowly. 'Try anything else again, or start acting too uppity, and your girl will get a lot more than a kick in her ribs or belly. Do I make myself clear?' Matt glared up at him and said nothing. Virgil groaned from atop Mirabeau's shoulder. 'We have a wounded man to tend,' Cantrell said, 'so crawl back to your blanket and stay there.' He turned on his heel and stalked to the other side of the fire; Mirabeau followed with Virgil.

Diana, who'd been watching, wide-eyed, expelled the tight breath in her chest and let the tension ebb from her willowy body as she watched Matt worm his way to his blanket.

Virgil moaned heavily as Mirabeau lowered him down on his blanket. 'Heat up some snow for water to wash his wounds,' Cantrell said. 'Then we'll bandage him up, and see if he makes it through the night.' Mirabeau moved away, took a pan and began scooping clean snow into it.

After Virgil's many wounds were cleaned, Cantrell doused them liberally with whiskey. Virgil squealed like a stuck pig. 'Reese, you're a-wastin' an awful lot of real good sippin' whiskey,' Mirabeau complained sadly.

'Gotta kill any infection. Now let's bandage him and move him away from the fire.' Cantrell corked the bottle and started to return it to his saddle-bags.

'Won't he freeze to death?'

'The cold will slow his blood, so he don't bleed to death. Had a deputy once who was gut-shot. Thought for sure he'd die on me before I got him back down the mountain. Turned out the freezing weather made the wound coagulate, and saved his life.'

'If'n you say so,' Mirabeau said with a shrug. As he began ripping up a clean white shirt, he nodded toward Diana and asked, 'Shouldn't she be doin' this?'

'Just 'cause she's a woman, that don't mean she knows anything about tending wounds,' Cantrell said dryly. 'Besides, she ain't got any feeling for Virgil. She'd as soon rub dung in his wounds.' He took a strip of cloth from Mirabeau and began bandaging Virgil's hand.

When they'd finished they moved Virgil and his gear away from the fire's warmth and left him shivering beneath his blanket. 'Now don't you up and die on us, Virgil,' Mirabeau said, 'or I'm gonna be plenty upset at all that whiskey gone to waste.' Virgil was too cold and delirious to reply.

★ ★ ★

Shortly before dawn the snow returned with a fury, driven before a shrieking wind. The flying flakes were thicker than before, blotting out the sky and mountains, and made travel impossible.

The wind brought a stronger chill than the previous day, and the group was forced to move their camp deeper into the sheltering pines. Cantrell cursed the delay which benefited only Virgil, who was in no fit state to ride.

As the snowfall continued throughout the morning, it became evident that their supply of firewood wasn't going to last through the day. Virgil kept slipping in and out of a pain-drugged sleep and couldn't be trusted to watch the captives. Cantrell refused Matt's offer to help with the firewood, and he and Diana were again tied to trees while Cantrell and Mirabeau spent hours hacking and dragging in firewood. Then the men checked on the horses and, brushing the snow off their backs, brought each horse into the area and walked it around the fire to restore its warmth.

The snow fell stubbornly into the night. The whining wind lessened, but was still with them. They bedded down as close as possible to the fire and curled up, shivering inside their blankets. Cantrell and Mirabeau took turns keeping watch on the prisoners and the roaring fire. The wind and Virgil's pained groans, whether asleep or awake, rasped on their nerves. Cantrell was sorely tempted to give in to Mirabeau's annoyed suggestion that Virgil should be put out of his misery.

The next morning they awoke to a silent world of sparkling whiteness. The wind and snowfall had stopped, and the sun cast its faint warmth out of a clear blue sky. Cantrell was restless and in a foul mood from too much physical exertion and too little sleep. Mirabeau's mood wasn't much better. The rest had helped Virgil who, while still in pain, was now coherent.

Matt came out of his sleep feeling strong and rested, and savouring the delicious aroma of boiling coffee. He'd made no effort to free himself, concentrating instead on getting as much sleep as he could. They were now only a couple of days from Vengeance, and he'd need all his strength and alertness for the inevitable showdown. He looked over and saw Diana stirring.

'It's about time you two decided to join us,' Cantrell said from across the fire.

Matt shifted to a half-sitting position and felt the frozen ends of his blanket tug as they broke free from the icy ground. 'How about sharing some of that coffee?'

Cantrell nodded and motioned to Mirabeau. 'Untie them.' The big man grumpily got up and moved around to Matt. 'Where's your manners, Mirabeau?' Cantrell drawled. 'Ladies first.'

'Well, shame on me!' Mirabeau muttered, and moved to Diana. The ends of her blanket were also frozen to the ground. He ripped the blanket completely off her and then knelt to untie her.

'Weather looks good,' Cantrell said to Matt. 'So let's try to make up for lost time today.'

'I'm game,' Matt said with a shrug.

He glanced to Virgil and casually added, 'But you got a hurt man, there.'

'He'll keep up. Ain't that right, Virgil?' The wounded man only groaned. Cantrell gave an unconcerned shrug and glanced to Mirabeau. 'Soon as you finish with them, go start saddling the horses.'

'All by myself?' Mirabeau complained.

'I'll be along to help you.'

'Yeah, after the work's all done,' Mirabeau muttered under his breath.

An hour later, they resumed their journey. Matt led the way, letting the dun pick its own way through the heavy snowdrifts. They rode to the edge of the forest and then, horses occasionally floundering, started across an open area leading above the timberline. Virgil clung to his pommel and groaned with every bump and jolt. Once he even fell off, and the group delayed till he agonizingly dragged himself back up into the saddle. Cantrell showed little compassion and kept scolding Virgil to keep up. The short man doggedly did his best. Matt now saw no reason to take them on any roundabout trail; Virgil was hindrance enough.

A little after noon, they climbed above the timber and found themselves in an eerie tangle of snowcovered rocks and great boulders. The sun reflected blindingly off the snow everywhere they looked. They were slowed by the horses slipping and stumbling on loose stones hidden beneath the snow. Once more Virgil fell out of the saddle.

'Aw, damnation, Virgil, can't you stay put!' Cantrell groaned, even though he and the others had been having a hard time staying on themselves.

Virgil painfully dragged himself to his knees, looked down at his bloody bandages, then paled and announced, 'I'm bleedin', Reese . . . '

Cantrell begrudgingly called a rest while Virgil was patched up. The rest was extended for lunch. When they were ready to leave, Cantrell ordered that Virgil be tied onto his horse.

'I ain't no prisoner!' Virgil indignantly protested.

'We're starting down the ridge,' Cantrell said. 'You fall off and you'll get to the bottom ahead of us — not to mention busting your wounds wide open.'

'That's a sure enough fact, Virgil,' Mirabeau said as he roped Virgil's feet in the stirrups. 'This is best fer you.'

They started up again and wound their way down a narrow trail in single file. Mirabeau now rode behind Matt, then Virgil, Diana and Cantrell brought up the rear. They reached the bottom of the ridge and began climbing the rocky spine of another mountain.

Here and there the sinking sun outlined the sharp profiles of escarpments and ridges in its fiery hues as the trail zigzagged across the grim faces of the peaks they rode and narrowed as they gained even more altitude.

Diana rode in almost a dreamlike state, weariness and the steady monotony of the buckskin's movement combined to blunt her senses. She hated mountain riding almost as much as she did Cantrell and his men. Great heights always gave her an emptiness in her stomach and a quivering in the back of her legs. Carefully avoiding the temptation to look over the edge of the trail, no matter how magnificent the view, she gripped her saddle-horn tightly and kept her eyes glued on Mirabeau's hulking form, massive in his buffalo coat. It wasn't an interesting view, but it was more comforting.

With every step his climbing horse took, Virgil groaned at the torture to his aching body. The groans came echoing back across the vastness separating the mountains, irritating the others. Finally Mirabeau turned in his saddle and glowered back at him.

'Dammit, Virgil, hush the hell up,' he snapped. 'You're a-spookin' the horses and gittin' on our nerves.' Virgil kept right on groaning. 'I mean it now, Virgil,' Mirabeau warned. 'You quit or

I'm a-gonna throw you right offa this here mountain and watch you fly like a rock!' Virgil wisely kept his suffering to himself. Mirabeau gave a firm nod, then turned around and resumed watching Matt ahead.

Dusk began to mantle the trail as the sun steadily declined. The trail broadened a bit and began to slope downward. It became colder as winds began playing tag across the mountains. Matt fretted silently. He knew they would have to find a spot for the night soon, before the trail became slick with ice. His concern grew as the sunlight became fainter.

Suddenly Matt's horse slipped. As he struggled to keep its head up, his eye spotted a wide-mouthed cave at the side of the trail. Had it been a bit darker he would have ridden past without noticing it.

They grouped their horses under a protective rocky outcropping and dismounted. Cantrell covered Matt and Diana with his Colt while Mirabeau freed Virgil from his saddle and helped him down.

'Looks like a real nice, deep cave,' Mirabeau commented, peering at the opening. 'We oughta be right warm in there.'

'Better take your rifle and go scout it first for critters,' Cantrell said.

'You mean bears and mountain cats?' Mirabeau asked uneasily.

'Could be,' Cantrell said dryly.

A dry stick cracked loudly under Mirabeau's boot as he stepped closer and squinted into the cave's interior. 'It's plenty dark in there . . . couldn't I just throw some shots around and see if anythin' complains?'

'And maybe kill us all with ricochets,' snorted Virgil. Mirabeau gave him a murderous scowl.

'Make a torch from some of this wood lying around,' Cantrell said, waving his free hand about at the scattered sticks around the cave.

'How'm I gonna hold a torch and shoot a rifle at the same time?'

'Virgil, you go with him and hold the torch.'

'I'm a sick man, Reese,' Virgil whined. 'I'm a-hurtin' awful bad.'

'You all stop carrying on like a couple of damned old ladies,' Cantrell said sharply, 'and get in there before we all freeze to death out here.'

Virgil made a torch and hesitantly edged into the cave. 'C'mon, Mirabeau,' he said, casting a glance back at the big man, 'don't be laggin' behind.'

'I'm right on your heels, Virgil,' Mirabeau said, cocking the Winchester.

'Well, you stay there. I don't wantta meet no varmints by my lonesome.'

His Colt not straying from Matt, Cantrell waited impatiently while the men explored the cave. A bit of time went by; still, there were no shots. At least they weren't going to have to fight over squatter's rights with some beast.

'Maybe they got lost,' Matt drawled, hunching his back against the icy wind that stirred around them.

'Don't you wish,' Cantrell said,

grinning sarcastically.

'We'd be a lot richer,' Matt said with a shrug.

'Well now, ain't you the greedy one?' Cantrell chided.

'You and me, we know the value of money,' Matt said slyly. He nodded toward the cave. 'Those two will just squander their shares in no time at all.' He paused, letting his words sink in. 'I never could understand why someone like you would saddle himself with such a sorry bunch to begin with?'

'You might not think much of them, but they're useful.'

'As cannon fodder?'

Cantrell smiled, half-amused. 'They do stand between me and others.'

'Your 'protection' is getting weaker all the time.'

'If the time comes that it's gone, you'll find me more than a handful.'

'I don't doubt that for a minute,' Matt said easily.

They eyed each other, eyes hard as stones belying their calm expressions.

Sure as the sun was going to rise tomorrow, both men knew that sooner or later they would clash, and only one would be left standing. Diana uncomfortably moved closer to Matt. Then Virgil's echoing voice broke the strained silence.

'It's safe to come ahead on, Reese. No critters anywhere!'

'You and Mirabeau make a fire,' Cantrell called. 'I don't favour losing these two in the dark.'

A few minutes later a fire brightened the gloomy cave, and Cantrell motioned Matt and Diana inside. They gratefully sat by the glowing warmth of the flames that licked upward, as though vainly trying to reach the cave's rock ceiling. Mirabeau pointed to the darkness behind them. 'This here cave goes back more'n thirty yards and narrows down to another openin'.'

'How big an opening?' Cantrell enquired.

'Enough fer a mountain cat to scoot in and out.'

'Or them?' Cantrell said, motioning down at the two.

' 'Specially her,' Mirabeau said with a nod.

'Then we'll have to watch them close tonight, won't we?'

'You mean we gotta sit up with 'em?'

'I mean exactly that.'

'Aw, Reese . . . ' Mirabeau objected.

'I don't wantta hear no back talk,' Cantrell cut in. 'Now tie their ankles, then Virgil will watch them while we haul in the gear and see to the horses.'

'He never gits to help with the chores.'

'I'm an ailin' man,' Virgil said quickly.

'Anybody dumb enough to run off by hisself at night a-chasin' wolves deserves to be ailin'!' Mirabeau growled, and lumbered off to fetch some rope.

* * *

The meal and pleasant warmth combined with the rigours of the day and brought drowsiness to the weary group. Virgil surrendered first, leaving Mirabeau and Cantrell to bind the prisoners for the night. Head pillowed on her saddle, Diana fell asleep on the hard, dry earth before Mirabeau had even finished tying her. He gently covered her with her blanket and returned to the fire. Cantrell joined him and they sat staring into the crackling fire.

'Guess it's up to you and me tonight,' Cantrell drawled, fishing the makings from a shirt pocket and beginning expertly to build himself a smoke.

Mirabeau scowled and jerked a thumb toward Virgil, asleep beside one wall. 'You mean he gits to sleep the whole night?'

Cantrell nodded. 'He needs all the rest he can get if he's going to keep up with us tomorrow.'

Mirabeau muttered an obscenity and spat into the flames. 'Couldn't we just bash them two over their heads so's they'll sleep through till mornin'?'

Cantrell frowned at his simple logic. 'You wantta chance addling Sutton's brain?' Mirabeau shrugged sheepishly. Cantrell finished making his cigarette and lit one end with a stick from the fire. 'I'll take first watch and stay awake as long as I can. Then I'll wake you.' The big man got up and shambled to his saddle, against the opposite wall from where Virgil slept. Cantrell sat savouring his smoke and watching the flames.

Presently Mirabeau's rasping snores spread through the cave. Cantrell was tempted to tell him to turn over but thought better of it. The commotion would certainly keep his mind off sleep. He smoked and let his eyes drift to the captives. Both appeared to be sleeping. The woman surely was; Sutton was probably laying there scheming. Let him. He'd ridden herd on enough men in the past, and Sutton was no different. There was no way he was going to skedaddle, not with the woman hindering him. Though he'd previously fought against thinking of her as anything other than a pawn to keep Sutton in line, Cantrell now allowed himself to speculate about her as a person. He didn't know if it was healthy or not, but, like Mirabeau's snoring, it helped keep him awake.

Sutton was one lucky man. He had a really beautiful woman who loved him something fierce. Cantrell idly wondered if she were capable of transferring that love, should Sutton meet with a fatal 'accident'. Once they started the digging in that mine shaft anything could happen. He grinned slyly as he thought on that possibility. He also thought how fetching Diana would look wearing that skimpy black costume of hers in mourning. He determined that he was going to see her in it as soon as they reached Vengeance. Funny, that was the first time he'd thought of her by name. It was a nice name.

Then he was sobered by the thought of how miserably he'd treated Diana up till now. There were some women who liked that kind of treatment, but he doubted she was one of them. It would be awful damned hard to overcome her hatred of him. Still, it might not be impossible. Breaking a woman was like breaking a horse. Once she accepted the fact that he was boss, he could let up and be gentle. Firm but gentle — that was the only way.

Cantrell blew a smoke ring and watched it drift up toward the ceiling. A long-suppressed memory began stirring in his mind. Thinking about Diana had brought it on. This time he allowed it to come through without immediately blocking it out. Maybe it meant a cleansing of the poison he'd been living with for the past six years.

He'd been a good sheriff. The townsfolk of Willow Bend had admired him for making the town fit for their families and bringing in more trade. But the one time he'd badly needed their help he sadly learned the difference between talking and doing. Sure, they thought he was a pillar of the community, but his job was too risky for anybody to gamble loaning him five thousand dollars so he could take his young wife back East for an operation. They were all mighty sorry about Betsy's brain tumour, but he just wasn't a good financial risk, earning only one hundred dollars a month and tempting fate every time he faced down a rowdy.

Then one day a new reward poster arrived. Jake Linder was sporting a five-thousand dollar bounty, and Cantrell decided he was the one to collect it. He said goodbye to Betsy and rode off for 'a couple of weeks'. It turned into a couple of months before he finally tracked Linder down. He put up one helluva fight, but Cantrell managed to bring him in alive. It took two months more to ride back to Willow Bend after collecting the money. Betsy was waiting for him — in the town cemetery. She had died a week after he'd left to hunt Linder.

It hadn't all been for nothing. He

found that bounty hunting was a whole lot more profitable than being a sheriff. From then on he hadn't given a damn about anyone or anything.

God, how he'd loved her.

Cantrell flicked his cigarette into the fire and let Betsy's lovely image form in his mind's eye. Despite the years, he remembered her just as plainly as if she were standing before him. He felt his heart quicken and his throat constrict. His eyes teared and he knew he couldn't stop them. He had to get away before his fragile self-control collapsed. No one must see him display weakness. Choking back sobs, he lunged to his feet and bolted from the cave.

Outside he shared his grief with the shrieking wind and let the tears, which hadn't come since that day in the cemetery six long years ago, burst forth freely.

13

Matt had discovered the sharp rock barely protruding from the hard ground when he'd first been tied. Under the cover of the blanket, his gloved fingers had dug away some of the packed earth to expose more of the sharp jagged edge. He'd been careful with his movements while Cantrell had been on guard, but now it was Mirabeau's turn. The hulking oaf was too busy trying to stave off sleep to pay much attention to him.

Careful to keep his body still, Matt watched the big man through slitted eyes and urgently continued sawing his wrist ropes across the jagged rock. Another strand parted. There was only one more rope left. He checked his movements as Virgil began moaning again. His wrists throbbed like hell and he felt like moaning right along with the wounded man. He watched Mirabeau shamble to the mouth of the cave, peer out into the darkness, then plop down against one rocky side. The fresh air didn't seem to help. Before long Mirabeau's head was again drooping to his chest.

Now Matt worked frantically, applying pressure with his arms and body as he dragged the remaining rope back and forth across the sharp edge. He gave a savage wrench and the partly sawed fibre snapped like a string. Matt winced as the blood slowly returned to his wrists, bringing a fiery tingling so intense that his eyes watered.

When he once more had complete control over his fingers, he drew his bent legs up closer to his body and began to pick at the knot holding his ankles. First, he had to undo the separate rope that had stretched between his wrists and ankles. The gloves made the task more difficult, and he was forced to stop and remove them. As he worked feverishly, keeping a wary eye on Mirabeau's sleeping hulk, he debated his next move. He could chance slipping over to Virgil, hopefully grab his gun before he could wake and then, if he was real lucky, shoot Cantrell and Mirabeau. He discarded the plan as too risky. With bullets flying around inside the closeness of the cave they might all end up dead. The best bet was to free Diana, get out the back of the cave and then work their way around to the horses while the men were scouring the cave for them.

The knot finally unravelled and Matt threw a cautious glance around him. Virgil was finally quiet and deep in sleep. Cantrell, on the other side of the cave, was asleep, his back turned. Mirabeau was beginning to snore in the mouth of the cave. The fire was fast becoming glowing embers, allowing the dankness to creep back out from the walls into the surrounding blackness. The less light the better. He eased from beneath his blanket and stole to Diana who was sleeping only a few feet away.

Matt crouched over Diana and pulled back her blanket to get at her ropes. Her wide eyes full of messages, she shook her head and urgently nodded toward the rear of the cave. He shook his head; he wasn't about to leave her. Yet it would take precious time to get her loose, then even more for her to get her circulation working right. There was no telling how long the men would stay asleep, especially Mirabeau.

Trusting that his newly restored strength was up to it, Matt scooped Diana into his arms and shakily drew himself to his feet. Normally she wasn't that heavy, but she felt like a boulder to his half-numbed body. He resisted the temptation to run and maintained his caution. There was no cry of alarm as he quietly, laboriously, made his way into the deeper blackness that was the passage leading to the rear of the cave. He remembered Mirabeau had said the tunnel narrowed and realized that he would need to feel his way along. He hoisted Diana over one shoulder and, with the use of one hand, began to follow one wall.

Presently, the passage made a bend and he saw a thin shaft of moonlight a short distance ahead. It seemed to grow as he approached. The rough walls closed in around him, but the passage was still almost wide enough for two big men to walk abreast of each other. He was tiring rapidly and, luckily, he wasn't long in reaching the hole. It was just as Mirabeau had said, large enough for a cougar to crawl through. He exhaustedly sank to his knees and lowered Diana down in the moonlight. He studied the hole and had serious doubts that a man in winter clothes could slip through it. Maybe if he shucked his coat . . . He'd find out soon enough, right now he had to get Diana untied. Turning her so her ropes were in the moonlight, he hastily went to work.

The knots were solidly secured and Matt found himself wishing he had the sharp rock he'd used to cut his own ropes. Diana lay passively, trying to keep her body limp in her bonds while he tugged, strained and pried at the stubborn knots. One by one the tight twists of rope begrudgingly parted and Diana was finally free, sitting up and massaging the blood back into her aching limbs.

Then an uproar came from the front of the cave, and they knew their escape had been discovered. Matt quickly helped Diana off with her coat and urged her toward the opening. She awkwardly obeyed and, stretching out on her belly, began to slither through the hole. Matt's heart sank as he saw it was a tight fit for her and realized he would play hell getting through himself. Running footsteps echoed in the passage and Matt hastily stripped off his coat as Diana's black leather-clad legs disappeared outside. He shoved both coats after her, then flung himself down and thrust his arms and head through the opening.

Dammit, even without his heavy coat the hole seemed too small for him!

Over his pounding heart and lungs he heard the echoing footsteps growing louder. He saw Diana, her concerned face pale in the moonlight, shivering in the cold as she watched his efforts. He squirmed and wriggled, desperately trying to force his broad shoulders through the constricting hole. She grabbed his hands and tugged. He gave an involuntary cry of pain as he felt the hard, unyielding rock sides scrape his shoulders. Diana instantly let go of his hands. Matt twisted and shoved, trying to compress his lean body, and managed to angle one shoulder partly outside. Encouraged by his small progress, he increased his straining efforts.

'Matt, hurry,' Diana cried, looking toward the trail as someone was heard crashing through bushes and ice-crusted snow.

Teeth gritted against the pain, Matt rolled on to his back. He had almost worked his other shoulder free when he felt a vicelike grip on his kicking legs, then a vicious yank dragged him back inside the cave. He found himself staring up at Cantrell, Colt in hand. Outside he heard Diana scream, then a struggle followed.

'Don't hurt her,' Cantrell shouted. The struggles came to an end and Mirabeau called:

'Want me to send her back through this hole?'

'Bring her around the other way,' Cantrell answered. As their departing footsteps crunched through the snow, Cantrell stepped back and beckoned Matt up. 'Awright, Sutton, let's go back and set by the fire. And don't get any fancy ideas about jumping me in the dark because Mirabeau will snap your girl's neck like a wishbone.' Matt stood and Cantrell shoved him forward and rammed the Colt's muzzle against his kidney.

Virgil had re-kindled the dying embers to life and the fire was crackling noisily, its leaping flames brightly lighting the cave's interior. No sooner did Matt and Cantrell emerge from the rear of the cave than Diana and Mirabeau entered from outside. The big man had Diana's struggling body slung over a brawny shoulder and carried the two coats in his free hand. He lumbered to Diana's bedding, dropped the coats, then smartly swatted her shapely bottom and unceremoniously deposited her on her blanket.

Angry and humiliated, Diana leaped up and swung a fist at his face. Mirabeau caught it in his huge hand and shoved, sending her backward. She tripped over her saddle and fell hard on her buttocks. He laughed in tolerant amusement, adding insult to injury. Virgil joined in. Diana sat seething, her large eyes radiating hatred.

'That's enough horseplay,' Cantrell said, his voice cold and menacing. He gave Matt a brutal shove that nearly flung him into the fire. 'Keep your gun on him, Virgil.' The short man obeyed and Cantrell turned gimlet eyes on Diana. 'I been too easy on you folks, and you've taken advantage of my good nature.' His quiet voice became chilling, 'Now get up, girl. It's time for another lesson.' Deathly frightened Diana involuntarily cringed at his tone.

'Cantrell . . . ' Matt began, a warning in his voice.

'Don't get sassy with me, Sutton. You got nobody but yourself to blame for this.'

'I'm who you're mad at, not her!'

'Mirabeau, shut him up.'

The big man stepped to Matt and swung a huge fist into his stomach. The air left Matt's lungs in a sharp, agonized gasp as he caved in the middle and crashed to his knees.

Diana leaped up with a scream and started for Matt. Cantrell caught her arm and swung her toward him. She fought madly, going for his eyes with her gloved fingers. He snapped his head aside and rapidly slapped and backhanded her across the face several times, then silenced her sharp cry with a fist to her taut midriff. Gasping, she sagged forward, only to be straightened up and hurled backward by a fist under her jaw. She collapsed like a rag doll at Cantrell's feet and lay still.

Matt gave a crazed yell and started to lunge to his feet. Mirabeau casually brought a hamhock fist down on the back of his neck, and Matt fell forward into a pit of darkness.

★ ★ ★

The morning was bright and clear, with the sun even hinting warmth, as the five plodded toward the summit of their climb. Behind them the timber-clad slopes receded rapidly until the treetops were a slanting, white-speared carpet far below. They rode in silence, listening to the tiresome sounds of the horses' hoofs on packed snow, their snuffling breathing and the creaking of saddle leather.

Matt's mind was on what lay ahead. He'd stalled about as much as he could. Sometime tomorrow they'd reach Vengeance, and unless something more happened he'd still be facing three men. On reaching the crest they paused to let the horses blow and, dismounting, looked down on an open saddle between two ascending ridges. In its middle was a large frozen lake, glistening in the sunlight.

'Appears we'd save time by crossing that lake rather than going around it,' Cantrell suggested.

Matt's hopes sank; this was his last planned delay. 'The ice might not hold,' he said, far too quickly.

'We'll find out when we get down there,' Cantrell said.

Several hours later they stood at the edge of the frozen lake. Cantrell stamped a boot on the icy surface and said, 'It seems hard enough.' The others looked uncertain.

'Maybe we oughta go around, Reese,' Virgil suggested.

'That'll take hours, it's less than a mile straight across.'

'I don't trust it,' Mirabeau said flatly.

'We'll test it,' Cantrell said easily. 'Mirabeau, ride out there a piece.'

'The hell you say!'

'You're the biggest. If it holds you, it'll sure hold the rest of us.'

'Supposin' it don't?' Mirabeau asked sceptically.

'We'll toss you a rope and pull you out.'

'Supposin' I sink first?'

'Then we'll always think kindly of you,' Virgil said, brightening at the thought. Mirabeau gave him a murderous scowl.

'Quit fussing and get on out there, Mirabeau,' Cantrell said impatiently. 'We'll be right behind you.'

'Yeah, *way* behind,' Virgil muttered.

Mirabeau hauled himself into the saddle and hesitantly prodded his horse out on to the ice. The others mounted, waited until the big man was about ten yards ahead, then cautiously walked their horses after him. Virgil lagged behind, ready to whirl his horse around and bolt back to shore at the first hint of danger. They reached the middle of the lake and resisted the urge to dash the rest of the way across. Things were going well, but Matt's nape suddenly got that familiar, unsettling tingle. He listened hard, straining for danger sounds over the chink of shod hoofs striking ice, and tried to tell himself that he'd had this feeling before and nothing bad had happened. He just about had himself convinced when there was a sudden ear-shattering crack.

The startled group looked back to see a long crack spreading toward them across the ice. It began veining out, loudly forming new cracks as it went. For a moment they sat gaping in heart-stopping dismay at the fast-approaching cracks shattering the lake's icy crust in web-like patterns. Then Mirabeau's terrified bawl stirred them into action.

'Every man fer hisself and the devil take the hindmost!' With that he slammed his heels into his horse's flanks and charged toward the bank.

The others came boiling after him.

It was a mad, helter-skelter flight with the chilling sounds of cracking ice pursuing them. They were nearing the bank when catastrophe struck Virgil. With not even a second's warning, his horse's snowpacked hoofs slipped on the slick ice. Man and animal went down with a bone-jarring *thump* and lay there for a long moment. The horse struggled to rise but its clogged hoofs refused to grip the icy surface. Virgil painfully sat up and looked about dazedly. The sight of the deadly crack racing toward him brought him scrambling to his feet with a yelp.

'C'mon, Virgil, run like a sumbitch,' Mirabeau bellowed from the safety of the bank. He wasn't foolhardy enough to ride back after him, and neither were the others tearing toward the bank.

Bringing up the rear and keeping a watchful eye on Diana, Matt heard Virgil's desperate pleas and glanced back to see that he had abandoned his vainly struggling horse and was slipping and sliding across the ice as the widening cracks relentlessly chased at his heels.

With a shrill scream, Virgil's horse disappeared beneath the ice. The crack overtook Virgil and ran right between his stumbling legs, parting the ice to either side. Arms flapping wildly to maintain his balance, the short, grubby man stood straddling the moving ice. Then, with sudden swiftness, he vanished down into the frigid waters and, through the ice, his dark, writhing shape was seen swept away by the current.

Matt urgently turned and rode like hell after Diana and Cantrell who were galloping up on to the bank. He reached its safety without a moment to spare. The four sat their wheezing mounts and gravely stared at the lake's shattered surface. Matt couldn't work up any remorse over Virgil, but he'd have preferred Cantrell or Mirabeau to have taken that last bath.

'You have your own impatience to

blame for that one, Cantrell,' he said dryly.

'Virgil was a hindrance,' Cantrell said callously. 'We'll make better time without him.' He squinted up at the sun. 'Still almost half a day ahead of us, so let's make the most of it.' He motioned, and Matt again took the lead.

The weather held, and the four riders passed the rest of the day without incident. Night found them camped at the foot of a long slope. On the other side lay Vengeance, and Cantrell and Mirabeau were bristling with restless impatience. With only the two of them left they were particularly watchful, adding other ropes to the captives' arms and legs, and checking them every hour of each man's watch.

Matt knew he had to sleep and gather his strength for tomorrow's ordeal. The long ride to Vengeance had taken its toll, just as he'd hoped. Unfortunately, the two men he was most concerned about were still alive. Tomorrow there would be only one way out — them or him.

*　*　*

They were up at the very crack of dawn. A tense excitement and expectation hung over the camp. Breakfast was bolted, and there was the hustle and bustle of breaking camp. Talk was almost nil, but Matt caught the uncertain glances Mirabeau occasionally gave Cantrell when he wasn't looking. It appeared, as Matt had hoped, suspicion was setting in now that they were near their goal.

In a little while they were in the saddle, and Matt led the impatient men up the long, jagged slope. Hour after hour they worked their way higher and higher. Then late morning found them on the crest. Below lay the ghost town of Vengeance, its heavily snow-layered rooftops sparkling and beckoning in the bright sunlight.

The long ride was finally over.

14

From a distance the ghost town had reminded Diana of a picture in a children's book. But as in fairy tales, when the shining palace suddenly turned ugly and sinister, the forgotten town lost its quaintness close up. Two long lines of rough-hewn buildings, roofs sagging under the weight of accumulated snows, stared forlornly at each other across the wide, snow-filled main street. Some were boarded up, others had broken windows and doors standing ajar. The horses' hoofs and creaking saddles seemed magnified in the funereal silence as she and the men rode along the empty street.

They put their horses into the rickety remaining stalls of an old livery stable, then took their gear and went in search of a building to camp in. They settled on the boarded-up saloon. After ripping away the weathered boards, Mirabeau put a brawny shoulder to the locked double doors directly behind the saloon's bat-wing doors and they flew open.

Even in its day the saloon hadn't been much. It was a hastily thrown-up rectangular building, practical and devoid of the standard gaudy elegance associated with most saloons. A rough-hewn bar dominated one side of the room. Behind it a long, dusty, broken mirror cast the group's distorted images back at them. A large pot-bellied stove occupied the middle of the room. Tables and chairs were scattered about and a roulette table and chuck-a-luck wheel stood on opposite sides of the room. A small makeshift stage took up the back area. A maze of cobwebs and thick layers of undisturbed dust attested that no one had set foot inside for many years.

'You oughta feel right at home,' Cantrell said pleasantly to Diana as he lifted her saddle-bags from across her shoulder. She favoured him with one of her iciest expressions. 'Mirabeau, bust up some furniture and make a fire. We'll eat and rest our bones a spell, then go find the gold.'

'Suits me,' Matt agreed, undaunted by Cantrell's meaningful stare. Then they were distracted as Mirabeau dropped his heavy saddle-bags to the floor, instantly raising a cloud of dust, and commenced smashing chairs like sticks.

'Now you go stand over by the bar and wait,' Cantrell said amiably. Diana started to move after Matt, but Cantrell caught her arm. She stared at him, her big blue eyes cold and questioning. 'I made myself a promise to see you in that black outfit,' he said, almost bashfully.

Diana's eyes widened incredulously. Then she said without emotion, 'Go straight to hell.'

'You want Mirabeau to lay a gun barrel across Sutton's snout?' Cantrell asked casually.

Fear flickered for an instant across Diana's exquisite face, then she nodded, resigned. 'I need someplace to change,' she said, and set her mouth tight with distaste.

'Mirabeau, keep an eye on Sutton,' Cantrell said, and led Diana toward a door on one side of the room.

Jaw set in anger, Matt leaned against the bar and glared after them. Mirabeau turned from stuffing wood into the stove and glowered at Matt, who tensed as Cantrell threw open the door and disappeared inside the room with Diana. After a few moments Cantrell walked out, closed the door and tossed the rope that had bound Diana's wrists on a dusty tabletop. Their eyes met and Matt choked down his anger. Mirabeau went back to feeding the stove while they waited.

The stove's heat was slowly chasing back the room's chill when the side door opened and Diana stepped out in her gambling costume. She paused for effect and forced a sullen smile as the men turned to her.

'Well now,' Cantrell drawled, 'I'd say this was worth the wait, wouldn't you, Mirabeau?' The big man grunted indifferently. Cantrell's eyes lingered on Diana. The brief, low-cut, one-piece theatrical costume, black fish-net stockings and slender high heels showed plenty of legs and cleavage, and emphasized her magnificent, statuesque figure. Her ivory skin and cascading golden hair were a vivid and intriguing contrast to the black costume. 'Come warm yourself by the stove,' Cantrell said cheerfully. Eager for the warmth, Diana didn't hesitate.

While the men were busy admiring Diana, Matt quickly palmed a shard of glass from the remains of a broken bottle scattered across the bar. He wasn't an instant too soon. 'You, too, Sutton,' Cantrell said. 'So we can keep a better eye on you.' Clutching the glass in his gloved hand, Matt ambled toward the group.

They sat in chairs placed around the

stove and had coffee and elk meat. Matt was able to conceal the glass between the fold of his coat and the chair seat. Diana was still the centre of attention and, as long as he made no sudden moves, Matt was only casually watched. When they'd finished, Cantrell looked over to Matt.

'How far's the mine from here?' he asked.

'About two miles.'

'We's gonna need somethin' more'n our hands to dig with, Reese,' Mirabeau said.

Cantrell nodded. 'I've been thinking the same thing.' He pushed himself up from the chair. 'Watch them while I go scout around town for digging tools.' Mirabeau nodded, content not to leave the warmth of the stove. Cantrell moved to the door, paused and looked back at Diana. 'Better do her up, and tie Sutton's legs too. We don't wantta lose these two now.'

'Damn straight,' Mirabeau agreed. Cantrell went out, and the big man begrudgingly roused himself from the stove. 'You set still,' he cautioned Diana, and walked over to the saddle-bags.

While Mirabeau was occupied, Matt hastily slipped the piece of glass out and held it up for Diana to see. She nodded, and he concealed it in his gloved palm as Mirabeau returned with some ropes and stopped beside Diana's chair.

'Awright, put your hands in back,' he ordered.

'I'd like to change first,' Diana said coolly.

Mirabeau shook his shaggy head. 'Reese might not be done a-lookin' at you.'

'You mean yourself,' Diana said, then sighed irritably and clasped her hands together behind the chair. Mirabeau snorted and leaned over her with the ropes.

Slouched in his chair, legs crossed and hands in his lap, Matt cautiously sawed the sharp glass across the ropes holding his wrists.

'Not so tight,' Diana complained, stirring in her chair.

'Stop squirmin' 'round while I'm a-tyin', and it won't be so tight,' Mirabeau growled.

Matt felt a loop part. There was only one more to go. Diana had to continue distracting Mirabeau until he was done. Then it would be up to him to take on the big brute.

As Mirabeau moved around in front of her, Diana subtly squirmed in the chair, drawing his eyes to her firm breasts which thrust boldly, due to her tied wrists and arms sharply pulling back her slim shoulders. His eyes took in what they were supposed to, and a couple of deep breaths helped keep his attention there. Then he forced his eyes away, dropped to one knee and began binding her tapered ankles together. Diana's eyes darted to Matt, who nodded, indicating for her to continue her distractions. 'Be careful,' she said crossly. 'Those stockings cost money.'

Mirabeau paused and squinted up at her. 'These here ropes ain't hurtin' 'em none, long as you don't go to strugglin'.' He again watched her bust rise and fall with her irritated sigh, then resumed his work. He cinched her ankles, connecting the end of rope to the chair's front rung, and stood. Diana wriggled, testing her ropes. 'Ain't no sense fightin' any knots I tie,' he smirked.

Diana tossed her long blonde mane and shrugged her bare shoulders. 'They're very secure. I'm certainly not able to harm you now.' Mirabeau's smirk became a scowl.

The rope parted and Matt's hands were free. He quickly flexed his fingers, stirring the blood back into his hands, then tensed as Mirabeau turned from Diana and approached, holding a length of rope in his right hand. He was almost to Matt before he noticed the severed rope and halted in mid-stride. The rope fell from his hand and he went for his Colt. Simultaneously, Matt hurled the piece of glass at Mirabeau's face and leaped up from the chair.

The big man howled his pain as the sharp glass embedded itself beneath his left eye. His draw was slowed by his free hand clawing at the bloody shard protruding from his cheek. Before Mirabeau could raise his six-gun Matt was on him.

Seizing Mirabeau's thick wrist, Matt pivoted and slammed his gun-hand against the side of the hot stove. The big man bellowed, dropped the Colt, and their scuffling feet sent it skidding across the floor, to come to a halt before Diana's bound feet. She took her large eyes from the struggling men, stared down at the six-gun and began fighting her ropes.

Mirabeau's huge left fist caught Matt on the side of his neck and knocked him reeling. With an enraged roar, he went after Matt. Through dazed eyes, Matt saw a big fist swinging down at his skull. He threw up a protecting arm and the heavy fist smashed down on his elbow, momentarily paralysing it. Another fist brutally caught him on the cheek and his head rode with the blow. His brain exploded with pain, blurring his vision with a red haze, and he felt his jellied legs trying to pull him down. Mirabeau grinned murderously and cocked back a right fist. Before he could throw the punch he heard the scrape of a chair and Diana's desperate, yet seething voice.

'Stop it, you filthy white trash scum!'

Mirabeau's head jerked toward her. Diana glared poison as her willowy body frantically twisted in the chair. He mocked her with a cruel grin. 'Hush your tacky mouth, girl, and just watch whilst I commence tearin' him apart.'

The momentary delay gave Matt time to somewhat recover and regain the use of his numbed arm. Mirabeau turned back to him and received a smashing right to the face that widened the cut on his bleeding cheek. The huge man rocked back on his heels. Again a fist crashed into his bloody cheek.

Bellowing his rage, he lashed out at Matt's face.

But Matt wasn't there. He heard Mirabeau's fist whisk past his ear as he dropped into a crouch and hammered both fists into his belly. Mirabeau's heavy coat absorbed much of the impact. Matt wheeled slightly and slugged him in the throat. The big man retched and stumbled back, his hands going to his aching throat. Matt moved after him.

Mirabeau suddenly recovered and both hands shot out, seizing Matt and squeezing him in a bear hug that lifted him off the floor. Matt worked an arm free of the crushing grip and hammered Mirabeau's head and shoulder. The big man tried to hide his face against Matt's chest. Lungs close to bursting, Matt desperately brought his other hand up under Mirabeau's chin and shoved his head back. Then he wildly beat both fists down on Mirabeau's upraised face. Staggered by the ferocity of Matt's attack, Mirabeau loosened his crushing grip. With a savage jerk of his body Matt tore free from Mirabeau's brawny arms and reeled against the bar. The big man crashed to his knees and, head lowered, arms limp at his sides, gasped for breath.

Diana's voice cut through Matt's grogginess and he squinted toward her. She urgently nodded down at the pistol laying before her feet, and he started toward her. Mirabeau recovered and lunged out as Matt passed near him. His long arms circled Matt's legs and tripped him to the floor. Matt landed hard and painfully. He managed to roll away from the pair of grasping, hamlike hands and regain his feet. The big man was up on his feet right after him. A blow caught Matt in the chest and knocked him back into his chair, upsetting it. Matt and the chair both went over.

Instead of taking advantage of the situation, Mirabeau decided he'd had enough and wheeled, heading for the Colt. Diana cried to Matt and tried to hitch her chair to the gun. Matt staggered to his feet, grabbed his chair and hurled it at Mirabeau. It struck the big man solidly on the back and brought him up short. Grabbing his spine, Mirabeau howled and sank to his knees. Matt charged forward, rammed an elbow into Mirabeau's ear as he passed and knocked him, sideways, to the floor. Diana stopped writhing and watched in relief as Matt scooped up the six-gun and whirled on Mirabeau.

The familiar feel of a pistol in his hand checked Matt's fury. At long last he was in control, and with a loaded gun he feared no man. Mirabeau lay curled semi-conscious, moaning and pawing at his various pains. He instantly fell silent at the deadly sound of the Colt's hammer cocking.

For an instant time stood still.

'Go on and shoot,' Mirabeau said, wincing in anguish, 'but Reese'll stop you from takin' the gold fer yourself.'

'There's no gold to take,' Matt said flatly.

Mirabeau shoved himself up on an elbow and gaped up at Matt. 'What'cha mean by tellin' such a lie to a dyin' man?'

'It's the truth,' Matt said solemnly. 'Pop McCarey and the others took all the gold back to Texas with them.'

'Why'd you say different?' Mirabeau asked indignantly. Then the light of understanding crept over his battered face and he answered his own question. 'You was a-tryin' to fox us.'

'That's right.'

'You still gotta git past Reese,' Mirabeau said belligerently.

'I'm going to have it out with Cantrell. But no matter how it ends, you're a dead man unless you show some sense.'

'Aw, you're just gonna bad mouth Reese to me.'

'For your own good,' Matt added, pivoting so he could see both Mirabeau and the saloon doors.

'Why would you be a-doin' me any favours?'

'It's for her,' Matt said, nodding to Diana, who frowned curiously along with Mirabeau. 'I want you to get her out of here and take her to the nearest town.'

'No, Matt!' Diana protested.

'Why should I?' Mirabeau asked, screwing up his bloody face in a surly, narrow-eyed scowl.

'Say Cantrell kills me: he sure won't need your help to take my body back for that five thousand reward.' Matt smiled coldly. 'You'll either get yours here, or somewhere along the trail.' Mirabeau's expressive face showed he was giving Matt's reasoning some hard thought. Matt dug his watch from his pocket with his free hand and held it up. 'This is engraved. You can show it to Goodsall as proof I'm dead and collect the reward.' He flipped the watch to the big man who clumsily caught it. 'That's if I kill Cantrell, or we kill each other.'

'Supposin' Reese kills you?' Mirabeau asked, opening the silver watch and checking the engraving inside.

'Then you keep the watch,' Matt said simply.

Mirabeau stared thoughtfully at the watch for a long moment, then snapped it shut and stuffed it into a shirt pocket. 'I'll do it fer you . . . and fer me, too, I guess.'

'Then start loosening Diana from that chair.'

Careful to keep his movements slow, Mirabeau stood and moved behind Diana's chair. Diana ignored him and fixed her arctic eyes on Matt. 'You men have forgotten one thing — me,' she said. 'And I'm not leaving here without you.'

Not wanting to waste precious time fussing, Matt said earnestly, 'I'm going to need a free mind when I face Cantrell. It'll be a lot freer knowing you're safe.'

'He's right, ma'am,' Mirabeau said helpfully as he finished freeing Diana's wrists and arms. 'Reese is plenty fast.'

'Oh, shut up and mind your own business,' Diana snapped peevishly, reluctantly accepting that she would be doing Matt more harm than good by staying. She brought her arms in front and chaffed her wrists while Mirabeau sheepishly came around and went to work on her tied ankles. She nodded and said in quiet resignation, 'We'll leave as soon as I've changed clothes.' She saw the relief on Matt's usually stoic face.

'Best change in the barn while I'm saddlin' the horses,' Mirabeau said, not looking up from his work. 'I promise not to look.'

Diana shot him an annoyed glance, but Matt said, 'Cantrell will be back any time, and I'd as soon not shoot it out while you're in here.'

'I'll fetch your things while y'all make your goodbyes,' Mirabeau said, tossing the rope aside and standing. He looked to Matt, who nodded in agreement, then headed toward the side room.

As Matt moved to her, Diana thrust herself up from the chair and clung to him fiercely. He held her and kissed her trembling lips. Caution made it a brief kiss, and his eyes warily returned to the saloon doors. He grimly knew there was a better than even chance he'd never see her again and he tried to put his feelings for her into words. They stuck somewhere in his throat. He settled for holding her and trying to convey that love through his touch and misty eyes. By the way she melted against him, Matt knew he'd succeeded.

They stayed that way until Mirabeau stomped out of the side room with Diana's clothes and saddlebags. Then they sadly parted.

15

Wearing her heavy coat and clutching her saddlebags and other clothes to her breast, Diana hastily followed Mirabeau along the backs of buildings to the livery stable. The sunlight failed to warm her black-stockinged legs and high-heeled feet which sank deeply into the snow with every step she took. As they came to the stable, they abruptly halted. One of the double doors stood partly open; both had been closed before. Nerves taut, they listened for sounds inside.

There was only silence.

Mirabeau turned and whispered to Diana, 'Wait here while I make sure Reese ain't rootin' around in there.' She nodded, her breath trapped in her chest at the thought. 'Keep watch till I beckon to you,' he added and, with all the stealth a big man can muster, cautiously moved to the stable.

As Mirabeau edged between the doors, Diana threw a nervous glance about the area and again thought of Matt. So far no shots had come from the saloon, which meant Cantrell hadn't returned yet. She desperately wished she and Matt could just ride away and leave Cantrell behind. But common sense told her the bounty hunter would relentlessly stalk their trail, and they would never be safe until Matt killed him or died trying.

Suddenly a sickening thud, followed by Mirabeau's horrid scream, jerked Diana's head back to the stable. She stared in confusion at a neat row of red-dripping metal tips protruding through the door that was ajar. Then it slowly creaked open wider and she gasped in stunned horror at the sight of Mirabeau's lifeless bulk impaled on the door by a rusty pitchfork.

There was movement inside. A dark figure appeared in the doorway. Gun in hand, Cantrell stepped out.

Eyes on the saloon doors, Matt stood beside the bar waiting for Cantrell to return. He held the Colt ready to fire the second Cantrell stepped through the doors. That wasn't quite sporting, but he and Diana had gone through way too much hell for him to be worried about the niceties of a gunfight. He abruptly tensed as Diana's distant scream reached him. Damn, Cantrell must have caught her and Mirabeau.

Matt pounded to the back door, throwing aside tables and chairs as he went, and rushed outside. Gripping the six-gun, he raced toward the stable, following Diana and Mirabeau's footprints. Then, through a cloud of his steamy breath, he saw the stable ahead and pulled himself up. Both doors stood open; Mirabeau was nailed to one with a pitchfork. Matt cautiously advanced, his sharp eyes straining to see into the stable's gloom. He was almost to the doors when a horse suddenly shot out carrying Cantrell and Diana's gagged, struggling form. Matt leaped aside, narrowly avoiding the charging horse, and rolled across the snowy ground.

'Meet me at the far end of the street,' Cantrell shouted as he galloped past and disappeared out on the main street.

Matt came to his knees, started to throw a bullet after Cantrell, but fear for Diana stopped him. He climbed to his feet, brushed the snow from his face and stood silently cursing fate. His edge was now gone. Cantrell knew he was armed and had called for a showdown. With Diana as hostage, Matt would have to face Cantrell on his own terms. Grimly, he started walking toward the main street.

* * *

Cantrell dragged Diana from the horse and shoved her back against a sagging hitching rail. As he quickly loosened her bound wrists, Diana brought a hand around in front and tried for his face and eyes with her long nails. He batted her hand aside, cracked a backhand across her gagged face, then yanked the coat from her body and twisted her arms behind her again. He tied her wrists and connected them to the hitching rail. Pulling his Colt, he pressed its muzzle painfully into Diana's side and looked back down the street.

Matt was nowhere to be seen.

'Sutton,' Cantrell shouted, his harsh voice startlingly loud in the silence, 'come on out and face me before your girl turns into an icicle.' He waited. There was still no sign of Matt on the long street. Cantrell cocked the Colt's hammer. Diana immediately raised her drooped head, her large eyes wide above the bandanna tied tightly between her teeth. 'If you're trying to sneak up and pot-shot me, forget it! I'll get your girl before I drop, and maybe you, too.' Diana stiffened and nervously bit down on her gag. 'I got all day,'

Cantrell continued. 'but she's already turning blue.'

'Here I am, Cantrell,' Matt called.

Shaking her dishevelled hair from her face, Diana turned her head and saw Matt's tall, lean figure stride out from between two buildings midway down the street. She felt the muzzle of Cantrell's Colt leave her aching side and glanced over at him.

Cantrell stepped back from Diana and, his eyes on Matt, began moving out into the middle of the street. 'I don't like being made a fool of,' he called. 'I was outside the saloon when you were making your deal with Mirabeau.'

'Why didn't you come barging in?' Matt asked, walking out into the middle of the street and halting, six-gun held down at his side.

'It was more fun to let you get your hopes up.' He nodded to Diana. 'And I didn't wantta risk her getting shot up.' He grinned coldly. 'I got plans for her.'

'You're not gonna live that long.'

'We'll see who's left standing after the smoke clears. How do you want this, Sutton?'

'Start walking and shoot whenever you feel you can hit something.'

'No fast draw, huh?' Cantrell chided.

Matt wasn't about to let himself be shamed into Cantrell's game. 'Nope,' he answered tonelessly and, raising his six-gun, started walking, ending further discussion.

'Either way, Sutton, you lose,' Cantrell said easily and ambled forward.

Oblivious to the cold air numbing her tall, briefly attired body, Diana stood rigid, her wide eyes glued on the advancing men. Lines of tension carved her smooth brow; her heart pounded madly, threatening to leap right out of her breast. This was the moment she had both prayed for and feared — and nothing could stop it. All she could do was stand and watch helplessly while the man she loved walked into a cold-blooded killer's six-gun. Diana's slim hands knotted into tight fists, nails digging into her palms, as a red flame blossomed from the muzzle of Cantrell's Colt, which leaped in his hand, and an instant later the booming shot echoed off the surrounding high-peaked mountains. Diana Logan flinched, her eyes on Matt. He was still standing. Frozen in heart-stopping fright, she watched the deadly scene unfold before her with a seeming slowness of motion that stretched each second into an eternity.

Cantrell cursed his impatience. His round had kicked up a small shower of snow about four feet short of Sutton's fast-striding figure. Undaunted, Sutton held his fire and kept right on coming. He was sure a cool one. Cantrell had hoped his shot would've brought a volley of rapid fire from Sutton, causing him to expend his shells before he got within close range.

The distance separating the men narrowed.

Cantrell squeezed off another round,

saw the slug rip out a piece of Sutton's heavy coat as it grazed his left shoulder but failed to draw blood, and again cursed his aim. Sutton came straight at him without a break in stride. The range was now just about right. Cantrell started to squeeze the trigger.

Suddenly flame and smoke belched from Sutton's .44. Something hard slammed into Cantrell's chest, jolting him back a step. It didn't hurt, but the pistol's roar confirmed that he'd been shot. A strange numbness crept up from his toes. It took his full concentration and every ounce of strength to raise his lowered Colt toward Sutton's chest.

Sutton's six-gun spat fire and smoke again.

Cantrell knew he was a dead man even before the second slug burrowed through his chest and spun his weakening body half around, dropping him to one knee. Damn it all, he wasn't about to die alone! He had to take Sutton with him, right now. But the

Colt felt surprisingly heavy in his quivering hand. In fact, his whole body was quivering. His blurring eyes caught sight of Diana, staring at him in silent horror.

No. It was *Betsy*. She was smiling, like he last remembered her on that day he'd ridden off after his first bounty. He had to go to her, tell her things were fine now. He was about to collect that five thousand they needed.

Every muscle straining, Cantrell drew himself up and, smiling through his pain, took a staggering step toward his Betsy. Why was she cringeing from him? Before his muddled brain could figure that out, a third bullet shattered his spine and hurled him face down in the snow. Betsy's image was lost in the cold, engulfing blackness as life left Reese Cantrell's body in a final shudder.

Granite-faced, Matt walked up to Cantrell's still body, kicked the Colt from his lifeless hand, then turned him on to his back with a booted toe and was surprised to see a smile on the bounty hunter's face. Probably just a death grimace that looked like a smile, he rationalized, staring down at Cantrell's slack-jawed face and wide, glazed eyes. Then he heard Diana's muffled cry and rushed to her.

Matt saw the love and great relief mirrored in Diana's exquisite face as he came up to her. Dropping his six-gun in the snow beside her coat, he put his arms around her and held her tightly. It was something he'd feared he'd never be able to do again. He felt her salty tears as Diana nuzzled his cheek and released her long pent-up fears in soft sobs. Matt spoke comfortingly as he quickly removed her gag and untied her, and drew comfort himself from the truth of his words.

The hell they'd been suffering through was now over. They were rid of Cantrell and his men and free to start living once more. Draping her coat about her shoulders, Matt led Diana away and left Cantrell's body sprawled in the middle of the snow-covered street.

The next morning they rode from Vengeance and continued on their way to California.

THE END

R